THE
MARRIAGE
I MOURNED

THE MARRIAGE I MOURNED

Book One

Sable Miles

Published by Sable Miles

Printed in the United States of America

ISBN: 978-0-9960080-4-4

*"Some secrets stay between husband and wife.
And sometimes they're shared."*

— Sable Miles

To everyone who showed up when it mattered — and to the ones who didn't. You both made me who I am. To every woman who has ever filed something quietly and kept moving. You know exactly what that costs. This one is for you. If you are here searching for hope or a way through, I want you to know you are not alone. Healing is possible, even if it starts out small.

Contents

Love is never any better than the lover.

— Toni Morrison

ONE
The Wedding

The day she married Rome, the sunlight felt like it had chosen them. The courtyard was warm with mid-afternoon light — the kind that settles softly over everything and makes even ordinary moments feel important. Chairs in neat rows. Flowers lining the aisle. The people they loved gathered, quietly waiting. From where she stood, it looked exactly the way she had always imagined it would.

Rome stood at the front, shifting slightly in his suit, while the last of the guests found their seats. He was handsome in the way that makes a woman feel chosen — tall, dark, with the kind of face that knew exactly what it was doing when it smiled. When he finally looked up and saw her, something in his expression changed. Not dramatically. Not the way they show it in movies. Quieter than that. More private. Like something in him had settled. She thought how strange it was that something so important could feel so simple.

When she reached him, he took her hands. They were warm. Steady. Their pastor, Reverend George

Wells, stood before them and began to speak. She barely heard the words. Her attention stayed fixed on Rome — on the particular way he was looking at her, like he already knew everything about her and had decided to stay.

That was the thing about him, early on. He made her feel chosen. Not in a grand way. In the quiet, deliberate way that actually means something. What she didn't understand then — couldn't have understood — was that sometimes the person standing beside you at the altar is already carrying something into the marriage. Not always a lie. Sometimes just a silence. A thing they know and have decided not to carry out loud.

That silence has a way of expanding over time. Filling in the spaces between you until it starts to feel like part of the architecture. But she didn't know that yet. That afternoon, in that quiet courtyard with the light resting gently over everything, she thought the hardest part was already behind them. She thought they had already done the work of becoming honest with each other. She thought that night was the beginning of her happily ever after.

The reception was loud and beautiful in its chaos — laughter, terrible singing, shoes abandoned beneath tables, aunts who had too much to drink and uncles who danced like they were trying to prove something. The room felt warm and alive. Her stomach hurt from laughing. At some point, she looked around and thought: *so this is my life now.* She liked that thought. She held onto it.

Wendy pulled her onto the dance floor — Rome's favorite cousin, loud and warm and impossible to say no to. Her best friend Stacey came with her. The three of them danced until her feet hurt, laughing at nothing in particular, the kind of laughter that makes a wedding feel real. She didn't know either of them well yet. She figured she had time. They were family now.

Rome was in his element that night.

She watched him move through the room the way she always watched him in spaces like this — easy, unhurried, like every conversation he walked into had been waiting for him. He had a way of making people feel like the most interesting thing in the room, and they loved him for it. His friends, his family, the people who had known him half his life — they all had a version of Rome they claimed, and every single one of them showed up that night to celebrate the fact that he had finally done it. Finally settled down. Finally chose somebody.

He chose her.

She knew what that meant to the people who loved him. Rome wasn't the marrying type — everybody in that room knew it, and most of them had probably stopped expecting it. But here they were. In their venue — the one she had opened the same month they got engaged, when it felt like everything she had ever wanted was arriving all at once. Surrounded by people who had watched them become something real, and the man who had told her once, slightly drunk and completely serious, that he couldn't play with God — that man had meant every word.

Rome came with history. The kind that had names and faces and complicated arrangements that predated her entirely. So did she. They were two full lives deciding to become one, and neither of them fully understood what that would cost.

And standing there watching him laugh at something David said — Rome's best friend — throwing his head back, completely unguarded — she didn't regret a single decision that had led her here.

At some point he found her through the crowd without looking like he was looking. Just appeared at her side, slipped his hand into hers, and leaned down close enough that she could hear him over the music.

"You good, Wifey?"

"I'm perfect," she said.

He smiled at her like he had never been surer about anything else. "Good. 'Cause you look beautiful. I just wanted to make sure you knew that."

Then someone pulled him away and he was gone again, back into the noise, and she stood there holding the feeling he'd left behind.

She had done big things for this man. Planned, shown up, given in every way she knew how to give. That was just who she was to him. She loved loudly, she gave without being asked, she showed up completely. Rome received all of it. Whether he deserved it was a question she had learned to stop asking out loud.

She knew the answer.

She just wasn't ready to let it change anything yet. She wasn't naïve. She wasn't blind. She saw the cracks even then — the little moments where he took more than he gave, the way he expected her effort like it was oxygen. But she had fire back then. The kind that made her say exactly what she meant, when she meant it. And if Rome had tried her on the wrong night, she would have made it clear—immediately—that she wasn't the one to play with. She wasn't the quiet version of herself yet. She wasn't the woman who swallowed things to keep the peace. Not then.

But marriage has a way of making you negotiate with yourself. And she didn't want to start over. Not again. Not with everything they shared.

By the time they finally made it back to the room, she was exhausted in the best possible way. The property sat just across from the venue. Their room was on the ground floor. When Rome opened the door, they were met with a surprise — rose petals on the bed, candles already lit. Jasmine had been there before them.

Jasmine was her best friend. She never really cared for Rome. Not once, not ever. She never understood what she called the hold he had on her. But she loved her enough to put all of that aside, and that room was the proof of it.

Rome stepped inside, taking it all in. She stayed in the doorway. He looked around the room, then back at her — still standing outside in the night air like she had no intention of moving.

"What's wrong, Wifey?"

She just stood there smiling. A little amused. A little tipsy. Waiting for it to click.

It didn't.

She laughed. "We just got married. You're supposed to carry me in."

"Ohh." The laugh that followed was real. "My bad, Wifey."

He came back to her, shaking his head, scooped her up, and carried her across the threshold. He kissed her and they both laughed.

Inside, the room finally felt like theirs. Her feet ached and the weight of the dress suddenly felt like everything she'd been carrying all day. Rome found the zipper along her back and worked it loose, kissing her neck as it lowered. For the first time all day, the room went quiet. No music. No crowd. Just the two of them standing in the soft light, finally alone.

She remembered thinking that this was the moment everything was supposed to begin.

As soon as her dress hit the floor, there was a knock at the door.

Then another.

They looked at each other, confused at first, then slightly irritated. He opened the door.

His cousin Jay stood in the hallway with his girlfriend, Harmony — bags in hand, visibly unsteady, wearing the particular expression of someone who knows they're about to ask for something they have no right to ask for.

"All the hotels are booked," Jay said. His words ran together at the edges. "We just need to crash here. Just for tonight. We can't drive like this."

He looked past Rome, at her; then quickly away.

There was a pause.

She had never met either of them before that evening. And now they were standing in the doorway of a room Jasmine had decorated for her husband and her.

Rome didn't say no. He didn't say yes. He turned and looked at her in a way that meant the decision had already been quietly transferred to her.

"Baby," he said. "They not from around here."

She took a breath. Thought about what she actually wanted to say. Decided it wasn't worth the kind of night that would follow if she said it.

"It's fine," she told them.

When everything in her wanted to say: hell no! Not tonight. Not this room. Not one single hour of this night. She didn't know it then, but this was the first time she shrank herself to keep the peace.

She pulled her dress back up.

The room that was supposed to feel intimate felt crowded instead. Later, lying in the dark with unfamiliar breathing filling the silence, she stared at the ceiling and told herself it didn't matter. One night. Marriage was bigger than one inconvenience. There would be other nights.

Right?

Rome rolled toward her — "You good?" he whispered.

"Yeah," she said.

And she meant it. Mostly.

She lay there for a long time after that.

Jay and Harmony's breathing eventually steadied into sleep. The candles Jasmine had lit were long out. The rose petals still scattered across the bed, slightly crushed now, surviving in spite of everything. Rome's arm was heavy across her waist.

She stared at the ceiling and did what she had taught herself to do — she reasoned through it. One night, she told herself. Marriage is bigger than one night.

Rome kissed her forehead in his sleep like he knew she needed it. She let it be enough.

They left for their honeymoon the next morning.

White sand. Blue water. Music drifting from beach bars after dark. They danced, drank, walked through unfamiliar streets holding hands, settling into the newness of being husband and wife.

It was easy in a way she hadn't expected. Uncomplicated. Light. One night on the balcony, Rome handed her his phone without explanation.

"Passwords, codes, everything," he said. "All of it. I'm all yours, Wifey."

She took it. Punched in the codes as he called them out. She needed to make sure they were real. Because he offered without being asked. A man who has something to hide doesn't do that. He was surrendering. Laying himself down in front of her completely. And she received it exactly like that.

In that moment, he became the man she had always been praying existed.

She was happier on that balcony than she had been standing at the altar.

The rest of the trip felt like that. Steady. Unhurried. Like the best version of them had followed them there, and the life waiting back home would feel just like this.

Celeste exhaled for the first time in longer than she could remember.

She told herself: this is it. This is permanent. This is the person she chose — the one she had decided to tell everything to, who had chosen her back.

She believed that.

For a long time, she believed that completely.

You are terrifying and strange and beautiful,
something not everyone knows how to love.

— Warsan Shire

TWO
Warning Signs

Before the marriage. Before the vows. Before Celeste had passwords or proof, there was them. Rome slid into her inbox the way men do when they've decided they want your attention and have chosen the path of least resistance to get it. A comment first. Then a message.

What she didn't know then was that Rome was exactly her type — Mr. All Wrong.

They had a mutual friend. Renee — her homegirl from back when Celeste was in culinary school. They usually stayed in touch through social media and hung out every now and again, but they hadn't spoken in years. When Celeste saw the connection, she reached out to Renee — casually, the way you do when you're not ready to admit you're already interested. Just asking. Just curious. Renee didn't hesitate.

"Celeste, girl, Rome is bad news. I know him from my old neighborhood. You know the type — got a woman or two or three. Girl, he a whole mess but he always been a cutie. You ain't gotta marry him. Just have fun — enjoy him for what it is, and don't expect nothing more."

They both laughed.

Celeste got off the phone and sat with that for a while. Longer than she admitted to anyone. She had just come out of a thirteen-year, on-again-off-again relationship — almost a marriage, almost a life, almost everything — and she was tired in a way that doesn't have a clean word for it.

But she couldn't do it. That wasn't who she was anymore. She still wanted the real thing. She still believed it existed, even after everything.

So she kept talking to Rome anyway. She trusted Rome with parts of her life most people never knew — the kind of truth you only share when you believe someone will protect it. That kind of trust should make a person careful. Reckless people don't always understand the value of what they've been given. The moment he openly accepted all of her, he made her believe he was the One — The Last One.

She remembered telling him once, very seriously, that he would be the last man she ever shared that part of her life with — the last man in her life, whether they made it or not.

She meant it.

Rome's acceptance meant something she couldn't name yet. It had nothing to do with love. It had everything to do with relief. Relief is a dangerous thing. It'll make you hold onto people longer than you should, just because they didn't flinch when you told them the truth. And Rome didn't flinch. Not once. Not even a breath.

That kind of acceptance hits different when you've lived long enough to know what it costs to explain yourself to someone new. She didn't want to start over. Not again. Not with everything they shared.

Looking back, she saw it clearly now. Rome accepted her. He just never saw why that should cost him anything.

They lived together for almost a year before they married. Those eleven months were the best time she remembered — not perfect, not magical, just easy. For the first time, she truly enjoyed being in his presence.

She started feeling safe.

He moved into her place in late summer. Even now she could feel that week — those evenings cooling while the air still held heat, the kind of weather that makes you believe transitions are gentle.

He brought two duffel bags, a television, and more confidence than furniture.

The house had been hers before it was theirs. She was a pastry chef at the convention center — early mornings, long shifts, the kind of work that follows you home in the best possible way. She had built a life in it before he ever walked through the door. But when he moved in she converted her guest room into a man cave. Gave him a space that felt like his. She didn't want him living in her house. She wanted them living in theirs. She had even customized a couch in his favorite team colors — it arrived the day before he did. She wanted him to walk in and feel chosen.

The house smelled like her detergent and the sage she burned every Sunday night.

When he walked in with his bags, it didn't feel like intrusion.

It felt like expansion.

At least that's what she told herself.

They laughed then — the kind of laughter that interrupts conversations and makes you lean forward and hold your stomach. He could turn burnt dinner into a dramatic monologue, a missed turn into an adventure, a long grocery line into a running commentary.

She mistook charisma for emotional safety.

She didn't know the difference.

One night, while he flipped through his phone, a face flashed across the screen.

"Scroll back," she said.

He hesitated, then did.

When the picture reappeared, her stomach tightened. She recognized her immediately.

"That's my cousin, Pam!" she said.

He frowned. "I don't know that girl, she hit me up."

"You might not know her," she replied, "but she knows you."

He shrugged. "She ain't never said nothing out the way. Come on now — y'all related."

"And we don't even speak anymore. If she's reaching out to you, it's for a reason."

He laughed. "You crazy. That's your family. Y'all need to chill."

"Delete her," she said.

"For what? It's just social media. You take this stuff too serious."

"You heard what I said, Rome."

"Man ok, you tripping for nothing."

She called Pam herself. Told her to stay out of his inbox.

Pam told her to stop being insecure and that she'd do what she wanted.

Celeste warned her not to go down that road.

She hung up.

Celeste asked Rome once or twice after that if her cousin had reached back out. He said no each time, so she stopped asking.

She took him at his word. Assumed her cousin had gotten the message.

She let it go. But something else was already there, waiting.

Brandi.

At first it was casual.

A show would come on and he'd say, "Brandi loves this one." A song would play and he'd say, "Brandi used to play this all the time." A restaurant commercial would prompt, "Brandi and I went there once."

She had never met her.

But she knew her name.

Too often.

She told herself she wasn't insecure. She wanted him to feel comfortable talking to her. She didn't want to be the woman who flinched at every female name.

But repetition changes meaning.

After the fourth or fifth time, she said something lightly.

"You mention her a lot."

He looked surprised.

"I do?"

There was no edge in his voice. No argument. He genuinely seemed unaware.

That unsettled her more than defensiveness would have.

If it was unconscious, that meant Brandi lived somewhere in his reflexes.

"I'm just saying," she added. "It's a little much."

He nodded.

"Oh. My bad."

And then he stopped.

Not because he had removed Brandi from his life — but because he removed her from Celeste's hearing.

Relief followed.

And relief is dangerous.

It convinces you the problem was small.

Once they got engaged, the language shifted.

We will. When *we're* married. After the wedding.

Commitment adds weight.

And weight reveals cracks.

He began stepping into other rooms to take certain calls. He started laying his phone face down.

Small things.

Small enough to explain away.

Privacy isn't secrecy, she told herself. Trust isn't surveillance.

She didn't want to be the woman who checks, who tracks, who needs codes.

She wanted to be secure.

Security built on limited information isn't security.

It's suspension.

Still, those months were good.

They stayed up late talking about wedding details, argued about guest lists, debated music, imagined the honeymoon.

He would say, "We're really doing this."

She believed him.

Because belief felt better than doubt.

And she held onto something Rome had said once, during one of those late nights when the liquor made him honest.

"One day… I'm gonna make you my wife."

He'd been drinking. That was usually when she believed him the most. There was something about the way inhibition left him that felt closer to truth than anything he said sober.

"But I wanna be ready," he continued, his words dragging slightly at the edges. "'Cause marriage is —"

"Marriage is what?" she asked. "Tell me."

"Marriage is serious," he said, nodding slowly like he was trying to convince himself as much as her. "I can't play with God. Oh no."

She laughed a little at how solemn and funny he managed to sound at the same time.

"Baby, yesss," he said, stretching the word out. "I know how much it means to you and I'm not ready yet."

"Rome, you ain't never gonna be ready," she said. "And I'm not going to wait forever."

He just looked at her and smiled — the kind that meant he wasn't worried.

This was maybe two years before he moved in — one of those circular conversations couples have when they're trying to figure out what they actually are to each other. She wanted to believe he was getting there.

For a moment, she did.

Back then, a moment was enough.

He gambled, smoked, drank too much — and she told herself those were just the edges of him, not the whole picture. Women messaged him — sometimes casually, sometimes in a way that felt a little too familiar. Conversations that lingered. Comments on his social media that made her pause. A comfort between him and certain people she couldn't quite place but couldn't quite dismiss either.

Nothing that amounted to proof. Just moments that sat with her longer than they should have.

In six years of dating, she never met the outside circle. Not really — just his close friends, the inner circle. Rome kept her carefully separate from the others, the ones he called "family," no relation.

She didn't know how much of it there was until after the marriage. His world opened up like a room she hadn't known existed, full of people with histories she hadn't been given access to, women who knew her husband in ways she was only beginning to understand.

When something felt off, she asked for clarity.

When a message felt too friendly, she called it harmless. When someone seemed too comfortable with him, she told herself she was reading into things.

She didn't want to be the kind of woman who interrogated every interaction. Rome was outgoing. People were drawn to him. She told herself that was just who he was.

That's the thing about warning signs. They rarely arrive as warnings. Most of the time they come quietly, dressed in something ordinary, easy to set aside if you're already committed to believing the best about someone.

And at that stage, believing the best about Rome was exactly what she wanted to do.

From the outside looking in, he was a good man. A good father who worked a remote 9-to-5 — in by nine every morning, on the road after that, nobody tracking his whereabouts but him. At the time.

He provided, showed up in the ways that are easy to point to. But he carried all of that quietly — not like something he did because he loved you, but like something he wanted acknowledged. To be his woman had a price. Sometimes it was the cost of looking away. Sometimes it was the cost of staying grateful for things that should have simply been expected.

When things were good between them, they were genuinely good. The kind of connection that's hard to explain to people who haven't felt it: easy laughter, comfortable silence, his liquor and her wine, no need to fill every moment with noise.

That kind of connection is dangerous. It makes you patient with things that don't deserve patience. It makes you believe that whatever is quietly wrong will eventually correct itself.

There was a night early on — a couples night out with David and his wife Kim — that she still thought about when she tried to explain what she meant about Rome and the way he moved through the world without considering the damage.

They were all laughing, drinks going, the kind of easy night that makes you feel like you've finally found your people. Rome was comfortable the way he always was with David — loose, unfiltered, performing for the room the way men do when they feel at home.

Then, out of nowhere, he leaned back in his chair, tapped David's arm, and said it.

"Remember when we used to date tens?" He shook his head like it was something to grieve. "Now look at us."

"Excuse me? I know you lost your damn mind," Celeste shot back.

Kim turned to David. "So you feel the same way?"

David didn't miss a beat. "Hell no. You're my ten. Always have been, always will be, baby."

Kim looked back at Rome. "I've seen some of the women you used to date, so calm down."

Rome laughed it off. Called Celeste sensitive. Said she was reading into things.

She filed it away, the same way she had started filing everything about Rome that didn't fit the version of him she was still trying to believe in.

She smiled. Finished her drink. Stayed the rest of the night.

That was the cost of being his woman sometimes. Not the big betrayals — those came later. It was the small ones. The ones he committed in front of people and then looked at you like you were the problem for noticing.

And so she stayed.

And looked away.

And explained things away.

And told herself the glimpses didn't mean anything.

But acceptance isn't the same as faithfulness.

He never stopped accepting attention from other women. And the glimpses she caught before they were married were never random.

They were warning signs.

When someone shows you who they are,
believe them the first time.

— Maya Angelou

THREE
The ENGAGEment

She thought they were celebrating him. That was the plan, as far as she knew it — his birthday, his night, his people. She had been working on it quietly for weeks. The food. The details. The particular kind of effort that says *I see you* without having to say it out loud. Rome had never had a birthday party as an adult, and she wanted to give him something that felt like proof of how seriously she took him. How seriously she took them.

She didn't know he had been planning something too.

The party was at their venue — hers, technically, though Rome had never been the type to draw that line and neither had she. She had started the business around the same time they got engaged, the same month. She poured herself into it the way she poured herself into most things she believed in. Event space. Decorating. The kind of work that lets you turn an empty room into something people remember. Rome had been there from the beginning. He had been there for the late nights and the early mornings, the bookings that fell through and the ones that didn't. So when she chose it for his birthday, it wasn't just a practical decision. It was a statement. *This is what I'm building. This is how I love.* Inside something she created with her own hands, she was throwing this man the party of his life — and he had decided to use it to change hers.

The room was full by the time they arrived — his family, his friends, the inner circle she had been slowly learning to navigate. Music. Drinks. The particular warmth of a room full of people who genuinely loved the person she loved. She moved through it feeling like she belonged there, which was still a feeling new enough to notice.

Until she introduced herself to one of his aunts. Celeste recognized her from a photo Rome had shown her once.

"Hi, I'm Celeste. Rome's girlfriend."

"Oh, you her. I thought it was someone else."

The woman looked her up and down and walked away before she could respond.

Celeste shook her head and said under her breath, *"and fuck you too, Auntie."*

She never mentioned it to Rome. She just made a note to deal with that aunt from a distance. The woman was too old to be that rude.

At some point in the night, Rome disappeared from her side. She didn't think much of it at first. Rome moved through rooms the way water moves — naturally, in every direction, pulled toward wherever the energy was highest. She got another drink. Talked to someone. Laughed at something she didn't remember now.

Then the music changed.

Then the room shifted in that particular way rooms shift when something is about to happen that most people already know about except the one person it's meant for.

Then Rome was in front of her.

He was nervous. She had never seen Rome nervous — not like this, not the real kind that lives in the hands and the jaw and the particular way a man looks at you when he has decided to be completely, vulnerably honest and is terrified of what you'll do with it. He took both of her hands. The room had gone quiet in the way rooms do when they're holding their breath on your behalf. He looked out at the room first — the way he always did, making sure everyone was with him.

"Y'all know me," he said, and a few people laughed because they did. "I don't do speeches. I don't do all that." He shook his head, smiling at himself. "But this woman right here — she loves to throw a party, so."

The room laughed. Someone hollered from the back.

Then he looked down at her. Just her. And the version of Rome that existed for everyone else quietly stepped aside.

"For real though." The smile softened into something she didn't see from him often. "You my best friend. That's real. You got my back like nobody I've ever had in my corner. You ride with me, you check me when I need it, you love me even when I make it hard."

His jaw tightened the way it does when he's fighting to stay composed.

"I love you with everything I got, Celeste. All of it. And I need everybody in this room to know that."

He reached into his jacket. Dropped to one knee.

"So make me the happiest man alive. Will you marry me?"

She said yes before he finished asking.

The room erupted. Someone was crying — she thought it was her. Someone was screaming, *yes!* Rome stood up and pulled her in, and the noise of the room closed around them like something warm, and she thought, standing there in his arms with everyone celebrating them, that this was what the waiting had been for. This exact moment. This exact feeling.

She held onto it.

Later that night, after the toast, after the dancing, after the room had thinned and softened into something quieter, Rome found her among the crowd, wearing an expression she couldn't quite place.

Not guilt. Not quite. Something more careful than that. The face of a man who has handled something and wants credit for handling it, but needs to tell you what the something was first.

"I need to tell you something," he said. "But I need you to hear me out before you react."

She looked at him.

"Tyra," he said. "She asked me for one last kiss. For old times' sake."

She was quiet.

"I told her no," he said. "And then she tried to push up on me anyway. I asked her to leave."

He said it like a man presenting evidence of his own goodness. And it was — she registered that. He had told her no. He had asked her to leave. He had chosen, in that moment, correctly.

But Tyra wasn't just an ex. She was connected to Rome in ways that predated Celeste entirely — and had used that connection to get herself in the room. Rome had said yes. And there she was. In the room. At his birthday party — their engagement party, as it turned out. She had stood among people celebrating their future and had asked her child's father for one last kiss. And somewhere in that same room, before Rome had done the right thing, Celeste had been floating on the best feeling of her life, completely unaware.

One of Rome's relatives nearby told her the rest. The way women sometimes share things without meaning harm. Tyra had apparently said it to more than one person before the night caught up with her: that she could take Rome if she really wanted to. That his being with Celeste was a choice, not a fact. That the door wasn't as closed as it appeared.

She was gone by the time Celeste knew any of it. Rome had made sure of that.

Celeste stood there for a moment, letting it settle. Then she took a breath, looked at the ring on her finger, and looked at the man in front of her who had, by his own account, done the right thing. Nothing could ruin that night. She meant that. The joy of it was too large for what Tyra had tried to drag into the room, and she was not going to hand Tyra the power to diminish it.

But she filed it.

Quietly, without ceremony, the way she had already learned to file things about Rome — carefully, in a place she could retrieve them from when she needed to understand the full picture.

Tyra. Memory bank.

The night ended the way it was supposed to end — with Rome and Celeste, the ring, the quiet after celebration when everyone had gone home and the moment finally belonged to just them.

Two days. That's all it took. Some people show you who they are before the ink on the certificate even dries.

— Sable Miles

FOUR

Newlyweds

For a few days, she held onto those feelings. The exhale. The steadiness. The belief that they had finally crossed into something permanent. They had been married just about two weeks when, one morning, his phone wouldn't stop vibrating.

Two messages. One after the other.

Ping.

Ping.

She was in the living room, television on her favorite baking show, his phone charging on the end table beside her. The bathroom fan was running. She could hear water hitting the tile. She stared at the phone like it might stop if she waited long enough.

It didn't.

Before the screen could go dark, she picked it up. The name at the top of the thread was Lisa.

She didn't know Lisa. She hadn't known there was a Lisa to know. That was the thing about Rome's world — it didn't reveal itself all at once. It opened gradually, one name at a time, each one arriving like a door she hadn't known existed until someone walked through it.

You left me hanging.

Her chest tightened. She shouldn't have scrolled. She did anyway. The thread opened like it had been waiting for her.

Hey. I'm back.

After that, the messages blurred together—not full sentences anymore, just bits that stayed with her.

Missed you.

Something about tasting.

Hungry.

Starving.

The messages were time-stamped the minute they docked. Her hands started shaking. In the bathroom, the water shut off. Rome was getting dressed.

Before she could think clearly enough to stop herself, she texted:

Well maybe because he's married.

Wasn't it your honeymoon, respectfully.

Respectfully —

That word hit differently than anything else in that thread. Not soft. Not apologetic. Sharp and unbothered, the way you speak to someone you don't consider a threat.

Two days after their honeymoon, her husband's mistress had just checked her through his phone.

And the worst part — the part she couldn't shake — was that she wasn't wrong.

"ROME!" Her voice tore through the whole house.

He came running. Stopped cold when he saw his phone in her hand.

"Celeste—"

"You texted her the second we docked?" Her voice was shaking and she didn't care. "The second you had service?"

"It wasn't even like that."

She laughed — sharp and humorless. "Don't play with me, Rome!"

"Wifey, just listen—"

"You texted her the second we docked," she added. "The second. You couldn't wait to get back to land before you went running to her."

He opened his mouth. She shut him down.

"*Respectfully,*" she said, "she got me fucked up!"

"Celeste, Wifey, listen it wasn't like that."

"Then what was it like? Because I'm looking at it, Rome. I'm reading it right now."

He stepped closer. "That freak bitch, if you had seen the stuff she was sending your husband—"

She cut him off.

Rome mentioned her only after he got caught. The way men do when they're trying to minimize someone by defining them — like giving her a label was the same as making her disappear. She was a freak, he said. Not someone worth losing a marriage over. He thought that would settle it. What it actually did was tell her everything about him.

"I would've what? Say it again," she said. "I dare you."

She didn't plan what happened next. He kept talking like she was fragile. Like she was emotional. Like she was the problem. And something in her snapped — not broken, just done.

"I was drunk texting," he said. "Me and the fellas was drinking—"

The decorative vase left her hand before the thought finished forming. It missed his head by a split hair and shattered against the wall behind him. Rome went completely still. She was already looking for something else to throw.

"Oh, you and the fellas." She gave a short laugh. "It's always you and the fellas when you're doing something stupid."

"Wifey, just listen—"

"You keep saying listen but all I hear is your bullshit, Rome." She was pacing now, her hands tight, her chest tighter from clarity. "You texted her the second we got off that boat. The second. Were you drunk then too?"

He ran both hands over his face. "You're blowing this out of proportion. I didn't do nothing with that girl."

There it was — the minimizing. This wasn't new. This wasn't sudden. This was who he had always been. And she had ignored it because she didn't want to start over. Not again. Not with everything they shared.

"That's not the point. You really think I'm stupid?" she asked quietly. "You really think I'm gonna sit here and let you play in my face?"

He swallowed.

Her voice dropped.

"You're my husband. We just got married. We just got back. And your first thought was her?"

She reached for the wine bottle. He reached for her.

"Wifey—"

"Don't touch me." She stepped back. "Get out, Rome!"

"Come on now, Wifey."

"Rome you're so embarrassing," she said. "We not even two weeks in and you already forgot that you're married."

His face shifted — not guilt. Annoyance.

That told her everything.

"Wifey, please. Not for her."

"Damn it!" He snatched his hat off his head, swung it through the air, then jammed it back on his head, cocked to the side."

He reached out to Celeste. She turned and walked towards the kitchen. He picked up his keys slowly, watching her like something in her face had surprised him.

She pointed toward the door. "You hungry, right? Starving? So go eat. Get the fuck out, Rome!"

"I'll be back, Wifey."

She turned. "Get out, Rome."

He walked out. The plate hit the back of the door and shattered before it had even closed.

The silence that followed was the loudest thing she had ever heard. She stood in the kitchen until the adrenaline left her body and took everything else with it. What replaced it wasn't calm. It was hollow. The kind of emptiness that comes after you've spent everything you had on something that didn't deserve it.

A while later, her phone lit up. FaceTime. Rome was at Wendy's. He tilted the phone slowly — showing her exactly where he was, who was present. Proof she couldn't argue with.

"Just gonna give you some space tonight," he said.

She nodded. She had put her husband out and didn't care. The house was quiet. That was enough.

They had made vows in front of everyone, what felt like days ago. They danced. They smiled. They had made promises in front of God and everyone they loved.

Two days.

That's how long it took for her husband to break the trust he had just restored on a balcony during their honeymoon. To make her look irrelevant to a woman she didn't know. To make her question everything she had believed, including her own judgment.

That night, she didn't sleep.

She was angry. Hurt. And underneath both of those, embarrassed. Embarrassed that she had confused transparency for faithfulness. Embarrassed that a gesture had been enough to make her feel safe.

"You can have it all, Wifey."

She had believed that. She had felt more certain in that moment than she had standing at the altar. Now she understood what it had actually been: not honesty, but confidence. The comfort of a man who knew what it took for her to trust him and had decided that was enough.

Access wasn't proof of loyalty.

It was proof of confidence.

The next morning she tried to shower, the water hot, steam filling the bathroom, rolling across the mirror and down the tile walls. She stood under the spray and didn't move.

She wasn't washing.

She was just standing there, replaying the word.

Respectfully.

It looped through her mind on a quiet, relentless circuit. Rome had let her look foolish to another woman within days of saying *I do*. And the woman on the other end of that thread hadn't been rattled. Hadn't apologized. Hadn't backed down. She had responded like someone who understood the arrangement better than Celeste did.

The tears came before she felt them. They ran down her face and mixed with the water, and for a moment she couldn't tell which was which. She pressed one hand flat against the tile and let both fall. She had believed him on that balcony. She had chosen him — specifically, deliberately, for reasons no one else knew and that he alone understood. He knew what trust cost her. He had accepted it all.

And then he had turned around and treated the marriage like something he could neglect without consequence. The feeling had been building since the night before, but there in the steam and silence, it finally overwhelmed her.

At first she thought it was the heat. But the floor tilted beneath her feet. The walls moved. Her stomach turned. She reached for the edge of the sink, trying to anchor herself. Her heart was racing and her breathing had come apart and she tried to step forward—

The room leaned sideways.

She slid down against the wall of the shower and sat there on the floor, the water still running over her, her body having decided it was finished before her mind had caught up.

She couldn't stand up.

She didn't know how long she stayed like that. But somewhere in the stillness, beneath the grief and the anger and the exhaustion, something else moved through her. Quiet. Barely a thought yet. More like the first cold edge of a feeling she didn't have a name for.

Not forgiveness.

Not fury.

Something steadier than both.

*Your body will tell you the truth your heart isn't
ready to speak. Learn to listen to it.*

— Sable Miles

FIVE

Aftermath

The floor was cold. She didn't remember crawling. She remembered the phone finally in her hand, her vision doubling when she tried to focus on his name. It rang once.

"Hey Wifey."

Her voice didn't sound like hers.

"Something's wrong."

No anger. No accusation. Just fear — stripped of everything else.

"I'm on my way," he said.

He was there in what felt like minutes. The same large, warm hands she had held at the altar were now lifting her off the floor. She hated that she leaned into them. That was the first moment she felt the shift — the quiet betrayal of her own body. She had gone from throwing vases to needing the same man who caused the storm to steady her. And that contradiction sat heavy in her chest, heavier than the dizziness.

He helped her dress. Helped her to the car. She stared out the passenger window the whole ride and didn't say anything, because there was nothing left to say that her body hadn't already said for her.

The lights in the emergency room were too bright. Even with her eyes barely open she could feel them pressing against her skull. Voices moved around her in fragments — questions, footsteps, the quiet slide of curtain rings along metal tracks. Her body felt like gravity had doubled. She tried to lift her head. It didn't cooperate. She tried to speak. Nothing came. Panic settled in slowly — not loud, just a quiet and terrible understanding that something inside her was no longer responding the way it should.

Near the doorway, she heard Rome's voice, low and uneven, on the phone with her mother.

"They think she might've had a stroke," he said.

Stroke.

The word moved through the room like smoke. *This cannot be a stroke. I just got married. I just got back from my honeymoon.* But her mouth wouldn't cooperate, and the ceiling lights kept blurring above her, and the only thing she could do was lie there and listen to other people speak about her body like it was something happening to all of them.

Her mom and Jasmine arrived together — worried, present, asking questions she couldn't answer. They didn't know about the fight. They didn't know about the messages or the word that had been looping through her head all morning. To them, she had simply collapsed. To her, she had collapsed for a reason, but she couldn't explain that yet. She could barely keep her eyes open.

Time stopped behaving normally. Minutes stretched. Voices faded in and out. A doctor leaned over her and asked her to follow his finger with her eyes. She tried. She didn't know if she managed it. The fear didn't arrive all at once. It came in pieces — first confusion, then frustration, then the quiet thought that if this really was a stroke, her life might never look like anything she recognized again.

The room grew quieter eventually. People moved in and out. Rome came back to the bedside, and though she couldn't open her eyes fully, she could feel his hand around hers. When it was just the two of them, he didn't speak. He just held on, like letting go might make something worse, and she didn't pull away. She didn't have the strength to decide what that meant.

By morning the tone had shifted. A different doctor came in — calmer, less urgent. The scans hadn't shown signs of a stroke. What they had found was something rarer, and in its own way stranger.

"A severe vertigo episode," he explained. "It can be triggered by motion sickness, dehydration, exhaustion, or extreme stress. Essentially, your brain and inner ear stopped agreeing on which way was up."

The room had literally been spinning. She had not imagined it.

"It should resolve with rest and time," he continued. Then he smiled — the small, diplomatic smile of a man about to say something he thinks is charming. "Though you two are newlyweds, so — no worries there."

Rome and Celeste looked at each other.

She rolled her eyes. He turned back to the doctor.

They gave it a fuller name later. Mal de Débarquement Syndrome. A medical way of saying your brain went somewhere and couldn't find its way back.

They had just gotten off a cruise ship. Under normal circumstances the brain resets within forty-eight hours of returning to land. But stress high enough to live in the nervous system acts as a barrier. The brain stays locked in motion. Still rocking. Still compensating for a ship that docked days ago.

Her body had been ready to come home. The stress of those first days back had kept it from getting there. Rome caused a storm she didn't know she was standing in.

Her body just kept the receipts.

It's amazing how your body will tell the truth long before your heart is ready to say it out loud. Hers had been whispering for months. Now it was screaming.

Relief after real fear doesn't feel like happiness. It feels like exhaling into a room that's still slightly wrong. Her body would recover. But lying in that hospital bed, weak and awake, she understood something that had nothing to do with the diagnosis. She had been lying on that shower floor thinking her life might be ending while the only person she wanted to call was the person who had caused it. That's the kind of thing you don't unknow once you've known it.

"She can't be alone," the doctor told Rome. "Someone needs to be with her until this stabilizes. Rest. Hydration. No stress."

"I'll be there, doc," Rome said, without hesitation.

He drove them home with one hand on the wheel, the other reaching over occasionally to rest on her knee. At home, he was careful and constant — steadying her when the walls tilted, bringing water without being asked, watching her from the doorway when he thought she wasn't looking. He didn't mention the messages. Didn't defend himself or revisit the argument. He simply stayed close and kept his hands ready, like the best version of him had arrived now that she needed it most.

Part of her wanted to tell him it was too late for that. But another part — the part that was scared and unsteady and exhausted — leaned toward him anyway. That was the beginning of the quiet version of her. The version that learned to survive by softening.

She tried to pull herself together, tried to sit up like she still had some control left in her body. But the room tilted again, subtle at first, then sharp enough to steal the breath from her chest. She reached for the edge of the mattress, pretending it was just a moment, pretending she wasn't unraveling right in front of him. It wasn't until he watched her try to stand on her own and sink back onto the bed that he broke. He crossed the room fast, his hands on her shoulders.

"Don't," he said, his voice cracking at the edge. "Don't try to do this alone."

He knelt in front of her. And then the tears came — not dramatic, not performed. Just quiet and guilty and real.

"I'm so sorry, Wifey. I didn't mean to hurt you." His voice was low. "She don't mean nothing to me. I swear to you. I love you."

She couldn't argue. She didn't have the energy to, and some part of her didn't want to. She reached out for him and they held onto each other at the edge of the bed and cried together, which was the strangest part. Because in her mind, he had caused this and he was also the one catching her, and she didn't know what to do with a person who could be both of those things at once.

The recovery weeks moved slowly. Her mom and Jasmine took turns sitting with her on the days Rome had to work, filling the space with quiet company and careful conversation. She told them enough. Not everything. Enough.

"Marriage is work," her mom said one afternoon.

"Men make mistakes," Jasmine added.

Jasmine had never liked Rome — but she wasn't the type to encourage divorce. She knew how much this meant to Celeste.

Celeste looked at both of them. She had watched their marriages for years — the long silences, the swallowed words, the compromises that didn't always look like peace but had to function as it.

"So I'm just supposed to act like it never happened?" she asked.

"That's not what we're saying," Jasmine said.

"You don't make permanent decisions when you're weak," her mom said gently. "Right now, your health comes first."

"He needs to help you," Jasmine added. "You can't even stand by yourself."

That landed. She hated that it was true. She didn't want him near her, but she couldn't even stand on her own. She didn't trust him, but she didn't trust her own body either.

So she stopped pushing him away.

The business was another thing entirely. She hadn't let it go — she had fought for it from that bed. Answering emails when she could sit up long enough. Taking calls with her eyes closed because the screen made everything spin. Rescheduling what she could, referring out what she couldn't. Some weeks she thought she was turning a corner. Two good days in a row and she'd start to believe she was coming back.

Then the room would tilt again.

And she'd lose another week.

And another client would stop waiting.

Eventually she had to let it go. The business she had just started building — the venue she had secured the same month he proposed — gone before it ever had the chance to become what she imagined. Not because she wanted to give it up. Because her body left her no choice.

For weeks she moved carefully — slowly, sitting more than standing, measuring every turn of her head. Rome adjusted alongside her, carrying things, driving everywhere, watching her when he thought she moved too quickly. Sometimes she caught him looking at her with an expression she couldn't quite place — like he was calculating something. Like he was trying to figure out if they were okay, or if she was just performing it.

He wasn't wrong to wonder.

The house felt different with him back in it. Not worse, exactly. Just different. Smaller. Like she was aware of every room and where he was in it.

She didn't feel newly married.

She felt alert.

Alert is a terrible way to live. It turns every room into a calculation, every silence into a question, every kindness into a negotiation. Once you start living like that, you never fully rest again.

*There are years that ask questions
and years that answer.*

— Zora Neale Hurston

SIX
Things Overheard

The bedroom had become her world. She wasn't steady enough to move through the house the way she used to, so most days she stayed there — pillows stacked behind her back, curtains half-drawn, the ceiling fan turning slow circles above her like time itself had slowed down. Rome moved carefully around the room. Quieter than usual. Softer. Bringing water before she asked, checking the clock for her medication, adjusting the blanket at her feet like precision could undo what carelessness had already cost. He was attentive. Present. Almost gentle enough to make her question what she remembered.

She was half-dozing when she heard the bathroom door click open. His voice followed a moment later — low, casual, the particular ease of someone who doesn't know they're being heard.

"...yeah, I know."

A pause.

"Alright... I love you too."

Her body went completely still. It wasn't dizziness this time. It wasn't sickness. It was recognition — the cold, clean kind that slices through denial like glass. Her body knew exactly what those words meant before her mind caught up.

He stepped out of the bathroom, phone in one hand, drying his chest with his free hand. He didn't know she had heard him.

"Who was that?" she asked.

He glanced up.

"Brandi."

Like it was nothing. Of course it was her. It was always her. The ghost in every room, the name that lived in the seams of their relationship long before the vows. She didn't say anything out loud, but the fire rose anyway — quiet, sharp, sitting right behind her teeth.

"You just told her you love her?"

He leaned against the dresser, unbothered.

"Come on now. That girl is like family."

"Your ex is like family?"

"Please don't make this bigger than it is," he added.

That sentence had history. It had been following her for years, dressed in different words, different tones, different excuses. Every time he said it, something in her tightened. This time, it locked.

Because she'd heard that tone before. She knew exactly where it lived. Years ago, back when they were still in their on-again, off-again rotation, they were sitting in his car outside her house one summer evening — windows down, music low, the air thick with heat and the particular tenderness of something new.

"I love you," he had said.

His words made her feel safe.

Then…

"I love her too."

The words didn't register immediately.

"Love who?"

"Brandi."

He said her name the same way he said everything — calmly, like she should have been expecting it.

"I don't think love has to be limited," he continued. "It doesn't mean I love you any less. I just love both of y'all. We could make it work."

"Make what work?"

"All three of us," he said. "Together. Nobody has to know. Just us. I wouldn't have to cheat. I would have the two women I love — I wouldn't need anyone else."

He said it like he was offering something enlightened. A more evolved arrangement. Like she should feel honored to be considered.

"What does Brandi have to say about all this?"

"She won't know," he said. "Just me and you."

He smiled. Patient. Like she was the one working through something.

"Just me and you? Oh, hell no!" she yelled. "So I'm gonna be the mistress in my own relationship?"

"Baby…"

"Huh, Rome? Are you serious?"

"You're thinking about it wrong," he replied.

And somehow, by the end of that conversation, she had walked away feeling unreasonable. Like wanting something simple and whole made her rigid. Like exclusivity was a failure of imagination.

The memory dissolved as quickly as it came. He was standing in their bedroom now, calling that same woman family, wearing the same patient expression he'd worn in that car. The past and present lined up so neatly it almost felt rehearsed. Same tone. Same logic. Same expectation that she would adjust herself around his choices. But she wasn't dizzy anymore. She wasn't confused. She was awake.

"You're married," she said quietly.

"Ok, I know," he replied. "That doesn't erase fifteen years of history."

No guilt. No hesitation. Just logic. Like the marriage was one fact among many, not the fact that changed all the others.

"She knows I'm married. She doesn't want me," he continued. "You're reading too much into it."

She pushed herself upright against the headboard, steadying her voice.

"I'm not reading anything. I'm hearing it."

He exhaled — long, slow, the exhale of a man who considers himself misunderstood.

"Celeste, don't do this right now. You should be resting."

There it was. Her weakness, repurposed as a reason to wait. Her illness, used as a timer on her feelings.

"Me being sick doesn't change what you said."

"You're emotional," he replied. "It's just words."

"It might just be words to you," she said, holding his eyes even though her body felt unsteady. "It means something to me."

He didn't apologize. He didn't argue. He just looked at her the way someone looks at a complication they've decided not to engage with right now. And walked out of the room. That was the moment something in her settled — not peace, not acceptance. Just truth. The kind that doesn't need to be argued or explained. The kind that changes the temperature of a marriage without making a sound. This wasn't a relapse. This was consistency. Rome had always believed that love didn't require exclusivity — only acceptance. The betrayal wasn't the words. It was how ordinary he made them sound. And how automatically she was expected to adjust.

It took three months for her body to feel like hers again.

Three months of holding walls. Of learning to trust her own balance. Of standing still until the spinning passed. Rome handled everything in the interim — bills, groceries, appointments, insurance calls. "Don't worry about money," he'd say. "We good. I got you Wifey." Rome was horrible with money. She had savings and credit cards that she used quietly, because she hated the feeling of being provided for by someone she wasn't sure she could trust. She hated that she needed him. She hated more that she was grateful.

He left in the mornings for work. Some days, he made stops that both of them knew he had to make. She had no good reason to question it and every reason not to push. If she doubted his schedule, she looked cruel. If she asked too many questions, she looked ungrateful. So she said okay and meant it, and said okay when she didn't, and eventually stopped being able to tell the difference.

David was Rome's best friend — married, settled. Home with his wife most evenings — but somehow still one of the stops on her husband's daily route. Her mom would cook on the days she came and Rome would cook or bring food on the others. This was only for about the first two weeks of recovery because they were driving her crazy. And they were scrambling her thoughts about fighting for her marriage.

From the outside it looked like a hardworking man, devoted husband, stretched thin between the people who needed him. But the mornings told a different story.

She started waking before him. Not deliberately — just light sleep, the particular shallowness that comes when part of your mind has decided it needs to stay half-present. The room would still be dim, curtains closed, and his phone would be glowing faintly against the nightstand.

She didn't know it was Brandi at first. Rome would call out a familiar name without looking at the phone — someone she'd expect. Like he was psychic.

The phone would ping between 6–6:15 a.m. Not once, not occasionally. Regularly. He always hid the contact name, flipping the phone face-down if he caught her looking. But one morning she was purposely sitting up by 6 a.m. just to see if she could catch a glance — and who else was it but Brandi. He hadn't noticed she was up until she cleared her throat on purpose.

"She's checking on my mom," he said one morning when he caught her staring.

She nodded.

That was the first night she went looking on purpose. Because something felt off. Because she already knew something was there. There's a difference between suspicion and certainty. By then she had certainty. She just needed to see it with her own eyes. If saying *I love you* to another woman in the bedroom your wife is lying in was nothing, she had to see what *something* looked like.

He knew she had all the codes but he never deleted Brandi. Like visibility made it innocent. Like if she could see it, it couldn't be a secret.

Two different times Brandi had asked him to pick her up from work while her car was in the shop. And he had done it. Both times.

She found out the second time it happened. Not because he told her. Because she read it.

She sat with it for a moment before bringing it up. She wanted to say it clearly — not screaming, not crying, just clearly — because this wasn't about jealousy and she needed him to understand the difference.

They were eating dinner the following night and she slid it right into the conversation like it was part of the weather.

"You picked Brandi up from work," she said.

He didn't even flinch. "Yeah. Her car was in the shop. What was she supposed to do?"

"Call a cab," she said. "Call an Uber. Call literally anybody who isn't my husband."

"You being dramatic."

"Rome." She kept her voice level. "You are a married man. You don't pick up your ex from work."

He looked at her like she had said something unreasonable. "She needed a ride. I helped her out. That's it."

"It was never just a ride."

He shook his head. "You want me to just leave people stranded?"

"I want you to understand that your first loyalty is to me."

He was quiet for a second. Then he said it.

"I never been married before."

She stared at him.

"And I have?"

"No—"

"Then that can't be your excuse."

He didn't respond.

And that silence told her everything his words were trying to avoid.

He never understood what he had actually done. And what he had done was simple.

Marriage isn't just a legal agreement. It's a declaration of priority. When you marry someone, you are telling the world — and more importantly telling them — that they come first. Not first when it's convenient. First. That means the people from your past no longer have the same access to you that they once did. Not because your spouse is insecure. Because access is a form of intimacy. And intimacy belongs inside the marriage.

Picking Brandi up from work wasn't a small errand. It was private time, alone, in an enclosed space, with a woman who had already made clear she considered herself family to her husband. It was availability. It was the message — whether Rome intended it or not — that Brandi could still call on him. That he would still show up for her. That the marriage had not fundamentally changed what he was willing to do when she asked.

A man who had never been married before might not understand that instinctively. But a man who loved his wife would want to. He would ask. He would think

about it. He would say *let me check with my wife first* —
not because he needed permission but because her
comfort was something he valued enough to consider.

Rome never considered it.

He just went.

And then looked at her like she was the problem
for noticing.

Something inside her went very still — not the
stillness of shock, but the stillness of a person who has
just confirmed what she already knew and is now
deciding what to do with it.

The pattern wasn't loud. It wasn't dramatic. It was
constant. And constancy can be more intimate than
desire. The woman after the honeymoon had been
hunger. Brandi was history. And history is harder to
compete with because it doesn't need to try. It simply
exists, woven into the fabric of a person in ways that a
marriage certificate can't undo. For the first time since
she'd gotten sick, she didn't feel fragile.

She felt aware.

Recovery, it turned out, wasn't only physical.
When your body slows down, your mind starts
catching what it used to move past — patterns, habits,
the small consistent things that only reveal themselves
when you finally go still. She knew where to look now.
And once you know where to look, you can't unknow
it.

Most nights, Rome passed out drunk before
midnight. When that happened, his phone was within
reach. She stopped looking when he was awake — he

interrupted too much. So she waited. And she started checking more frequently — not frantically, not desperately, but methodically. The way you check a wound you already know is there. And whether the finding was small or significant, there was always something.

She watched the easy familiarity between her husband and his "family" — the kind of intimacy that looks harmless to anyone who doesn't understand what it means to still talk to an ex that way after you've said vows. The casual shorthand. The unguarded warmth. Things that take years to build and don't go away just because a marriage happened.

Then one message stopped her entirely.

She had to read it twice before her mind would accept what her eyes were already telling her.

Rome had written:

I need you to help me get out this marriage.

The moment you start keeping count, you've already lost faith. The moment you stop keeping count, you've already lost yourself.

— Sable Miles

SEVEN
Always Something

A sharp pain moved through her chest. He wasn't asking Brandi how to fix their marriage. He was asking her how to leave it.

Brandi replied almost immediately.

Why? What she do now?

Celeste stared at the screen.

What she do now?

Like this was a running conversation. Like she had already been reduced to a recurring complaint he brought to another woman — a problem he narrated to her in real time while Celeste slept beside him.

Rome had responded:

She driving me crazy. I can't breathe in here.

Something in her went still. Not shocked — just confirmed. He wasn't venting. He was confiding. And he wasn't confiding in her. Brandi was his outlet — the place he went to hide from the truth of his own life.

After that, Brandi went quiet. For a few days the thread settled. Then the pattern resumed — simple texts, early mornings.

Good morning.

No hearts. No flirting. Just consistency. The kind that said she woke up with Celeste's husband on her mind and saw no reason to stop. And that consistency was what bothered Celeste most. Desire burns out. Habit doesn't.

Now every time the phone pinged too early in the morning, she was asking Rome:

"Who's that?"

Only now it was everybody except Brandi.

Again, without looking at the screen — "It's David."

"At six in the morning?"

"Yeah." A pause. "What's wrong with that?"

She studied him. Not the words — the ease. The way he could lie without blinking. The way he could make her feel unreasonable for noticing what he was doing in plain sight.

"Nothing," she said. "Just didn't know y'all had that kind of bromance going on."

He turned his head toward her.

"So now you jealous of my best friend too?"

"Too?" She looked at him. "Who else am I jealous of?"

He let out a short laugh. "Wifey, you think everybody want your husband."

"No," she said evenly. "I think my husband wants everybody."

His face shifted.

"You tripping."

"Make sure Brandi knows to text at more reasonable hours."

"That girl don't be texting me no more, like you wanted."

"Okay," she said.

"It's too early for this." He sat up and grabbed his phone, heading for the bathroom without another word.

"Well, you heard what I said," she called after him.

He came out, got dressed, sat in his man cave for a few minutes, then left for work early without much of an explanation. She didn't argue. She had already stopped caring enough to.

Later that morning, she checked his location. He wasn't at work. He was at the casino. Of course he was. Rome always had a way of choosing escape over accountability. And somehow she had become the one expected to pretend it was normal. She looked at the screen for a moment, then set her phone face down on the nightstand. She didn't say anything when he came home. Some information you file away rather than expose your full hand.

David had a wife and a home of his own, but Rome still moved through his house like nothing in David's life had changed. So she started checking his location the way you check a thing that has lost your trust.

One afternoon the dot wasn't at David's. It wasn't anywhere she recognized.

She didn't say anything when he came home. She sat with it instead — let the information settle, gave herself time to understand what it meant or if it meant anything at all. By then she had developed a way of holding information quietly. Not burying it. Just filing it.

Rome came home late that night, already drunk. He'd been drinking with David — that was his answer before she asked. They settled into the man cave, his space, his show. This was their quality time together and he pulled up an episode of *Cheaters* he'd apparently been saving.

A man. An ex who never left. A girlfriend who already knew but needed to see it.

She glanced over at Rome.

"This is exactly what I'm talking about. You and your ex."

He smirked at the screen. "But he don't even want her."

The irony sat between them like a third person on the couch. He could watch another man's mess with full confidence while sitting inside his own.

Then, casually: "I knew you'd like this one."

She turned to look at him. "So you've seen it before?"

"Yeah. Earlier. On my phone — at work."

She held his gaze for a moment. Work had never appeared in his location that day. Not once.

"You're really sitting here watching this with me," she said slowly, "while you're doing the same thing."

He didn't even blink. That was the part that hit her — the ease of it. The man could sit beside her watching another woman get disrespected while doing the same thing to his own wife.

"How many times do I have to tell you I'm not doing nothing wrong?" He shook his head. "Wifey, you got yourself a good husband."

"Good at what, cheating?"

"I ain't never cheated on you!" He was on his feet now, voice raised, something reckless moving behind his eyes the way it always did when the liquor and the guilt got loud at the same time.

"I have a phone full of messages that say otherwise."

"If you would just stay out my phone, we wouldn't even be having these problems."

"No! If you would stop acting like you're single."

"Bitch, please — I wear my ring every day."

"What?"

He caught himself. Looked at her.

"My bad. My bad, Wifey. I didn't mean that."

He reached for her. She stepped back.

"Don't."

He looked at his phone. Stood up from the couch. Lit a cigarette. And then, in the particular way that drunk men sometimes say things they've been holding — not in anger but in careless disclosure, like the words had simply been waiting for an opening.

"I got bitches asking me, 'Why you marry her ugly ass over me?'"

The room went quiet.

Not because everything stopped.

But because she did.

Ugly.

The word didn't cut — it echoed. Not because she believed it, but because he had carried it home. Because he had chosen to repeat it. Because somewhere in him, it had landed enough to say out loud.

She sat with the word for a moment. Let it land fully. Because it deserved that — not to be deflected or minimized, but to be held up and looked at clearly. Her husband had just carried another woman's words into their home, into their marriage, into her face — and delivered them like a man reporting news he had no part in.

"So you think that's something you should say to your wife?" she asked.

He shrugged. "I'm just telling you what they said."

As if the repetition made him innocent. As if choosing to bring it home — choosing to say it out loud, to her, in their house — wasn't its own kind of answer.

Something snapped. Not dramatically. Quietly, the way things snap when they've been under pressure long enough.

She stood up and walked toward him, tears slipping down her face. She needed to see the man behind the vows — the one who could speak love and practice disrespect in the same breath.

"Who do you think you're talking to?"

He didn't flinch. Didn't soften. Just stood there with his beer, unmoved, like she was weather he was waiting out.

"See, this is what I'm talking about," he said. "You keep accusing me of cheating, and I'm out here turning bitches down."

She wiped her face. "I have never been disrespected like this in my life."

He looked her dead in the face. "Well, it's a first time for everything."

She walked to their room.

She closed the door behind her.

She sat with the anger until it dulled enough to breathe through. The argument ended. The word didn't. It lingered in the room long after he passed out. It sat on the dresser, in the doorway, in the silence between them. Words don't disappear just because the person who said them is too drunk to remember.

Ugly.

It moved through the quiet of the room, settling into corners she hadn't thought to guard. It hit differently coming from her husband — not because she believed it, but because he had chosen it. He hadn't defended her. He hadn't laughed it off or left it with the women who said it. He had picked it up and carried it home to her, and the question she kept returning to, sitting alone in that room, was whether that was carelessness or something more deliberate.

A drunk tongue speaks a sober mind. She had heard that her whole life. She just never thought she'd have to apply it to her husband.

Did he actually think she was ugly? Was it the vertigo? Was it the stress? Did this man even like her? She didn't have an answer yet. But she was starting to understand that she needed to start asking better questions.

About an hour later, she went to the kitchen. On her way, she glanced into the man cave. Rome was passed out on the couch. Snoring. The cigarette he'd lit was burned down to nothing in the tray beside him.

She left him there.

She didn't speak to him for days after that. When they finally did talk it was surface level — necessary exchanges, nothing more. He started coming home and going straight to the cave. Sometimes he slept there. The distance between them didn't feel like a fight that hadn't finished. It felt intentional.

When you don't set boundaries, you give people permission to determine your worth.

— Iyanla Vanzant

EIGHT
The Cycle

After about a week or so, they were back to normal — or whatever passed for normal by then.

His phone buzzed early one morning beside the bed.

"It's five in the morning. Who is that?" she asked.

"I don't know," he mumbled without opening his eyes.

The phone buzzed again.

"Who. Is. That?"

He glanced at the screen.

"It's just Brandi."

"Oh," she said calmly. "So she's still texting crazy hours."

"I can't control what she do."

"Okay."

And she left it there.

She had gotten good at leaving things there. It was a skill she hadn't known she was building until she looked back and realized how many things she had simply set down and walked away from. Not because they didn't matter. Because some things you don't have to pick up to win. She took a breath, took her time, and got up.

She showered. She made a cup of coffee and sat at the kitchen table with her phone. She opened a new message. Added Rome. Then added Brandi. Her thumbs hovered over the screen. She typed. Deleted it. Typed it again.

She was tired. Tired of Brandi. Tired of Rome. Tired of pretending she didn't see what was right in front of her. So she waited until Rome left for work. Then she read the message one more time and pressed send.

For a moment nothing happened. The message just sat there between the three of them.

Then her phone buzzed.

Brandi replied.

Rome and I are FAMILY. That's not changing. You his wife, right? Try worrying about your marriage instead of worrying about me.

She read it again.

FAMILY.

The word landed wrong. Not because Brandi said it — but because she believed it. Like she held a position in his life Celeste was supposed to respect.

Like Celeste was the one intruding on something Brandi thought she belonged to.

Something in her snapped. She called Brandi. Texting suddenly didn't feel direct enough. The phone rang once. Twice. Then voicemail. Brandi didn't answer. So she texted.

You're right. He chose me as his wife, and I ain't never standing for him playing in my face. I'm not offering up my friends to keep him comfortable either.

And Rome, since you want Brandi to help you get out of this marriage, let her start by getting your shit out of my yard. The fence will be unlocked. Brandi, come get your family out of my house.

The message showed delivered. Then seen.

But unanswered.

Silence has a sound when people know they're wrong. It's the quiet that follows a truth they don't want to touch.

Rome never replied either.

That silence told her everything — not one of them was willing to stand in the truth she had just put in front of them. Three people in the same conversation. Nobody willing to say anything else.

Her coffee had gone cold, which pissed her off even more. She took a sip anyway. Outside, the morning moved like nothing had happened. Cars passing. People heading to work. Everything ordinary.

Except her marriage — that was unraveling in real time while the world kept moving like it didn't notice.

So she slowly packed up Rome's belongings and put them in the backyard — no need for the neighbors to know their business. She didn't have to wait long.

Rome always came home. No matter what happened, no matter what she found or what they argued about, he still came back through that door. And somehow that kept her locked in. Like choosing home counted for something. Like the man who kept leaving pieces of their marriage scattered everywhere was still the same man she believed had chosen her. But that didn't matter anymore.

When he finally walked in, he smelled like liquor before he even spoke. He stumbled toward her and tried to kiss her. The audacity of affection after disrespect always hit different. Like he thought access was automatic. Like her body was still his even when his loyalty wasn't.

She pulled back.

He paused.

Then the excuses started before she even said a word.

"It wasn't like that, for real, wifey. If you would just stay out my phone—"

She looked at him.

"Oh," she said slowly. "So that's the problem?"

"No. Yeah."

"What?"

"No, no—" he said quickly, his words slurring together. "Wifey, I'm sorry."

He always apologized like the words were currency — something he could spend to buy his way back into the version of them he kept breaking.

"Rome, your stuff is out back. Call Brandi and let her know you're ready to go."

And right on cue, the tears started.

She sighed.

"Rome, cut the shit. It's old now."

He straightened up immediately.

"It's old?" Standing at the back door, he looked at her. "Why would you throw my stuff outside?"

She just let her eyes say what her mouth didn't.

"Wifey, look," he said, rubbing his hands over his face. "I know you're sick of me, but it's been a lot. You get sick, the bills, all this about these women who don't mean nothing to me, with everything else going on."

She sat quietly and listened.

Rome leaned closer. He was right up in her face, slurring and spitting. He was disgustingly drunk.

"You my wife," he said. "I love you. I married you."

He said it like a shield. Like the title itself was supposed to protect him from accountability. Like loving her in theory excused everything he did in practice.

"But you want out, right?" she said calmly. "So go."

She meant it. For once, the sentence didn't shake on the way out. It felt like truth, not threat.

"No. No, wifey."

He shook his head.

"I'm here. We're here together. I love you and I swear I'm going to do right by you."

He kept saying it.

Wifey.

Like the word itself was supposed to fix everything. And the truth was, sometimes it worked. The way her husband said it softened her more than she liked to admit. It had a way of pulling her back in, reminding her of the vows they made.

For better or worse. Right?

She looked at him.

"Rome," she said sternly. "You're a broken record."

And the truth was, she knew every word of the speech before he even said it. At some point she had fooled herself into believing this was just a part of marriage — the arguing, the apologies, the tears, the promises to do better.

So she watched him bring his stuff back in. At some point she got up and helped — picking up what had been sitting in the yard, carrying it back through the same door she had put it out of. Neither of them said anything while they did it. There was nothing to say that hadn't already been said. They just moved through it together, piece by piece, until the yard was empty and the house looked the way it always had. It was muscle memory at this point — the choreography of leaving and returning, breaking and repairing, hurting and pretending it didn't hurt. They knew the steps too well.

Like nothing had happened.

Like that was just what they did.

It wasn't until later that week that she called her therapist for the first time in months. She had been in therapy before Rome — stopped somewhere in the middle of them, the way you stop doing things for yourself when you're busy trying to hold something else together. The vertigo had brought her back.

Her therapist called it situational depression, which was a clinical way of saying her body had started keeping score before her mind was ready to admit there was a game being played. The antidepressants helped level the floor beneath her. Therapy helped her understand what she was standing on.

That afternoon she called her therapist. Not in crisis. Just to say out loud what she hadn't said to anyone else.

"I think I already know how this ends."

Saying it out loud didn't make it real. It just made it harder to ignore. Her therapist didn't try to talk her out of it. That was why she kept going back.

Brandi fell back like a ghost in the night. One minute there, the next gone. Her boyfriend was very thankful for the new information.

And with her gone, the house got quiet in a way that felt almost unfamiliar — like the air finally had room to settle again.

For a while after that, things were genuinely quiet. Not the tense kind of quiet where you're waiting for the next thing — actual peace. Rome came home on time. They cooked together sometimes, his playlist on low, both of them moving around the kitchen like two people who had figured out how to share space without taking up too much of each other's. They went out. Stayed in. Laughed at things that had nothing to do with them or their problems. There were whole evenings where she forgot to be alert. That was the danger — the softness that came after the storm. The part where you start believing the break in the chaos is the healing, not the warning.

She had promised Rome she would stop throwing him out if he promised to honor their marriage. And for that stretch of time, it felt like they were both keeping their word.

And when a pattern finally pauses, even briefly, your body wants to believe it's a turning point, not just another calm before the next hit.

She let herself rest inside it. Carefully. The way you rest when you're not sure how long it will last but you're tired enough to take it anyway.

But this man, her husband, wouldn't allow them to get through one situation before he was putting them in another. A few months after the Brandi group text, there was already someone else. With Rome, the calm was never an ending — just an intermission.

Things had been feeling a little off. Rome was going to the casino, then coming home and asking if he could go back — like he hadn't just been there. Like the first trip hadn't happened.

She never let on that she knew. His location had always been her one quiet advantage, and somewhere along the way he seemed to forget it existed.

She'd watch him construct a story with such confidence, and sometimes she'd laugh to herself. Sometimes she'd shut it down without explanation. But she never said too much. Never showed her hand. That was the thing about Rome. He always thought he was ahead.

He rarely was.

The first thing that caught her attention wasn't the news the woman was sharing. It was the way she addressed her husband.

Babe!

Some woman named Kelly was calling her husband *babe.* The familiarity of it irritated her more than the word itself. Kelly wasn't guessing her position — she was confident in it.

She kept scrolling. They had been texting every day. In one conversation, Rome mentioned how much bad luck he had been having.

What Kelly replied next stopped her cold.

Babe, do you think it's because you're married and messing with me?

She read it again.

Messing with me?

Not texting. Not talking. Not friends.

Messing. With. Me.

There it was — the part he never admitted but always acted out. The truth women tell each other when men won't.

The phone nearly slipped out of her hand. Her whole body went hot — the kind of hot that starts in your chest and floods everything else before your brain can even catch up. She wasn't sad. She wasn't hurt. She was furious in a way that felt like something cracking open inside her that she would never fully get closed again.

She scrolled faster. Hands shaking.

Rome asking if Kelly wanted to meet up after he finished checking on his mother. Kelly saying yes without hesitation. Back and forth. Easy. Comfortable. Like Celeste didn't exist.

Then she saw it.

Happy Birthday. From her husband. To Kelly. With plans to meet at the casino. His obligations didn't stop him from making lunch dates. And this explained the big floral arrangement he had walked in with for her that same day — flowers she had accepted with a smile, not knowing they were guilt wrapped in cellophane. She had thought he hit big at the casino. Apparently he did.

She put his phone down. Walked to the kitchen doorway. Rome was at the stove, moving around like a man with nothing to hide, humming something low under his breath. The smell of food filled the whole room. He had no idea she knew. That was the part that burned — the ease of his double life, the comfort of it, the way he could hum over a stove while her whole body was vibrating with truth.

And she stood there for a moment watching him — her husband, cooking her dinner. Like he hadn't been messing. With another woman.

She went back to his phone.

She pressed the call button before she could think about it.

Kelly answered on the first ring.

"Hey babe—"

The word hit her like a slap.

"Hey who?"

Silence.

Dead, complete silence.

Then the line went dead.

She called back. Kelly didn't answer. Called again. Straight to voicemail. So she texted her from his phone.

You're sleeping with my husband but won't answer the phone?

Nothing.

"ROME!"

Her voice tore through the whole house. She heard him moving before she even finished saying his name. Footsteps, then the man cave doorway, then him stopping cold when he saw his phone in her hand.

What happened next wasn't clean. The real kind of argument — the kind that has been building for months underneath ordinary conversations and almost-normal days — doesn't stay contained. What came out of that room wasn't one argument. It was every argument they'd been having since the honeymoon. It was all of it at once, finally using its full voice.

Rome denied everything he could still deny and deflected everything he couldn't. She said things she meant. She said some things she didn't. At some point the wall between what was said and what was done dissolved entirely and she was just in it — present, raw, too tired to perform anything resembling calm.

What she remembered most clearly was afterward. The aftermath always told the truth. Not the yelling. Not the chaos. The quiet. The way two people sit in the ruins of what they just said and pretend they can still build something on top of it.

The house going quiet. The particular sound of a room after something has broken. Rome sitting at the kitchen table with his hands around a glass he wasn't drinking from. Celeste at the counter with her back to him, staring at the window, watching the light outside like it was something she could hold onto. They didn't talk for a long time. When they did, it wasn't about what had happened. It was about what happened next.

After this situation with yet another woman, she restructured things. Rome had money for the casino.

Money for other women. So she put all the household bills in his name. Every one of them. They had split everything before that — they had a vision, they had plans and dreams. That arrangement ended the day she found those messages. He hated it. But the math was simple: if he had spending money for other women, he had bill money. That was the new arrangement. It wasn't revenge. It was balance. If he wanted the freedom of a single man, he could carry the responsibilities of one too.

Life adjusted around it the way it always did — quietly, without asking permission. They went through the motions. She went to work. He went to work. They came home to the same house and ate in the same rooms and slept in the same bed and did all the things that look like a marriage from the outside. From the inside it felt like two people waiting to see which one of them would finally say what they both already knew.

Neither of them said it.

Instead they tried — or something that looked like trying. There were better weeks. There were weeks when she caught herself genuinely laughing at something he said, genuinely relaxing into an evening without keeping score or staying alert. There were moments that still felt like what they were supposed to be. And she held those moments carefully, because they were easier to hold than everything she was trying not to name.

That was the strangest part. Even in the middle of something that was clearly not working, there were threads of something real running through it. The connection wasn't gone. The feelings weren't fiction. They had something — she just didn't know what to call it.

Something real can still be wrong. Something genuine can still cause damage. Loving someone doesn't require you to stay in a life you know you don't deserve and isn't yours. She didn't understand that yet. Not fully.

She was still trying to find a version of their marriage that would last. But every version required her to shrink. And she was starting to outgrow the places she kept folding herself into.

*Have enough courage to trust love one more time
and always one more time.*

— Maya Angelou

NINE
The Reset

The first year of their marriage had already been heavy. Lisa had surfaced during the honeymoon. Brandi appeared while she was still recovering. Then there was Kelly — the one who called him *babe*, who wondered whether his bad luck was God's way of weighing in on their arrangement.

Three women. One year. And somehow they were still standing. Standing didn't mean stable. Sometimes it just meant neither of them had said the words out loud yet. Celeste wasn't sure what that said about either of them. So she did what she always did when she ran out of answers.

Before their second anniversary, she had set up a counseling session with Reverend Wells. Rome was against it from the start — he didn't believe in counseling. But he showed up.

She had spoken with the pastor beforehand — enough that he understood what they were walking into. He didn't soften it when they met privately. He told her straight out that Rome was behaving like a man who wasn't ready for marriage, and he asked her

— with genuine concern — whether the stress of the relationship had played a role in how long she stayed sick.

She didn't disagree. Her body had been telling the truth long before her mouth ever did.

But she told him what her mother had always told her. You try once. You try again. And then you try one more time. When you've done all you can do and there's nothing left to give, that's when you leave with a clean conscience. She wasn't there yet. She still had pieces of herself she hadn't exhausted trying to make this work.

Reverend Wells listened. Then he sat across from both of them and read scripture, speaking quietly about keeping the marriage between the two people in it — leaning on each other and on God rather than letting outside voices fill the space that belonged to them. At one point he addressed Rome directly. Celeste watched her husband's jaw tighten. Then slowly, his eyes filled.

One tear. Just one. He wiped it quickly, like he didn't want anyone to see it. But she saw it. And she let it be enough to pull her right back in. Hope is a dangerous thing when it's tied to the smallest gestures. A tear can look like change when you're desperate for a sign.

And she was desperate for something to point toward progress, even if it was small.

After all, they were there to save what could be saved of their marriage. Right?"

So when their second anniversary approached, the idea of renewing their vows felt right. Not a ceremony — just something small and intimate. A way of saying they were still choosing each other. Rome didn't seem excited at first. He kept bringing up money.

"I'm not trying to spend all that on another wedding," he said.

She looked at him, confused because her credit cards had taken just as many hits as his, if not more, the first time around.

"You think I want a whole ceremony?" she asked.

He shrugged. Once she explained it would just be something simple, his mood shifted. When he suggested inviting David and Kim, he was suddenly on board entirely.

"Oh," he said. "That's different."

Rome always performed better with an audience.

She noted that. Filed it quietly, the way she filed most things about Rome. Her memory had become its own kind of protection — a place to store the truths she wasn't ready to confront out loud.

The truth was simple: her husband needed an audience to show up for his own marriage. Without David and Kim in the room, recommitting to her wasn't something that excited him.

She let it go. They were trying. And he settled back into himself after that, the way he always did once he realized she wasn't pushing the issue anymore.

She called Reverend Wells a few days later and asked him to officiate.

He declined. Gently. Without saying why. But she knew why. She had seen it on his face in the counseling session, heard it in the things he had asked her privately. A man who believed in the marriage would have said yes. She knew that, sitting in her car after she hung up. She knew it and she kept going anyway.

So Celeste planned a small trip — three days, just enough to get away from the house and the routine and everything that had settled into the walls around them.

The morning of the renewal started quietly. The hotel room was still dim when she woke up, curtains half open, winter light turning everything gray. Rome was still asleep beside her — one arm stretched across the bed, breathing steady, looking like a man with nothing on his conscience. She watched him for a moment. There was something about seeing him like that, unguarded and still, that made everything feel almost simple. Almost simple was the closest they'd been to peace in months.

She slipped out of bed and walked to the bathroom, careful not to wake him. The floor was cold.

She turned on the shower and stood watching the steam rise while everything from the night before settled back into place.

Renewing their vows was supposed to mean something. A reset. A recommitment. A way of saying that whatever had been coming apart between them could still be repaired. She wanted to believe that. Standing there in the quiet of that bathroom, she admitted something to herself that she hadn't said out loud yet.

This wasn't just about love anymore. Love had stopped being the anchor. Hope was doing all the heavy lifting now. The particular kind that lives in the space between who someone is and who you still believe they could be. Hope that the man she thought she had married was still somewhere inside the man she had been arguing with. Hope that if they both said the words again, something inside the marriage might realign. Hope that commitment, repeated sincerely enough, could be stronger than everything working against it.

She wanted to believe vows could fix what behavior kept breaking.

When she stepped back into the room, Rome was sitting up rubbing his eyes.

"You ready?" he asked.

She looked at him for a moment.

"Yes," she said. And in that moment, she meant it.

The renewal itself was small — just the four of them, standing together, repeating words they had already promised each other once before. She remembered looking at Rome while he spoke his vows, trying to read his face. Trying to decide if he meant them. Trying to decide if she believed him even if he did.

At the time, she wanted to.

That night the room held only the sound of the ocean and the particular silence of two people who had just said forever again and weren't sure what to do with it. Rome reached for her in the dark — not urgently, not the way he reached when he wanted something. Slowly. Like he was asking a question he didn't have words for.

She answered. They always spoke the same language in this space. Whatever they were outside of it, in that space, they were still something. Something familiar. Something dangerous. Something that felt like love even when it wasn't safe. Something she hadn't figured out how to let go of yet. Because that's where their truth was centered.

Afterward he pulled her close and she let him, her back against his chest, his arm across her like an anchor. The waves kept coming outside. She stayed awake longer than he did, listening to the water and wondering how long borrowed peace was supposed to last.

She was still deciding. But the decision was already forming in the quiet parts of her — the parts that had stopped believing his tears and started believing her own exhaustion.

The cooking challenge had been David's idea — each person responsible for one dish, something to contribute to a big shared breakfast. It turned into exactly what you'd want from a trip like that: loud opinions, friendly arguments about technique, Rome holding a spatula like he'd invented the concept of breakfast.

He made French toast.

It was good. Really good. They all said so. Rome looked pleased with himself. He always glowed under praise — especially the kind that made him feel like the man he pretended to be.

They had a full day after that — excursions, drinks, the kind of easy fun that makes you forget for a few hours what you came here carrying. By the time they got back to the room they were both exhausted. They passed out before the night was over.

She woke up in the middle of it needing water. Rome was still asleep. She padded to the kitchen, grabbed a bottle of water, and picked up his phone as she got back in bed.

Brandi. Good morning texts, every day since they'd arrived. And somewhere in the thread, Rome telling her how much he loved her French toast. Asking how she made it. Saving the recipe she sent back.

She set the phone down. The betrayal wasn't the recipe. It was the intimacy of it — the quiet exchange, the shared moment he brought into their marriage like it belonged here.

The French toast he had made that morning — the one they had all praised, the one he had accepted compliments for with that easy smile — was her recipe. Celeste had eaten it. Called it delicious. Watched her husband beam over a recipe that wasn't his.

She put his phone back. Lay there in the dark beside him. The waves were still coming outside. Rome was still breathing steady, one arm stretched across the bed, completely unaware. The trip changed after that.

Once you see the truth, you can't unsee it. Even if you spend the last day pretending you're okay.

They argued — more than once, and not quickly — but David and Kim were there, so they managed themselves. They smiled when they needed to. They performed normal when the situation asked for it. Performing had become second nature — the mask they both wore so no one would see the cracks they were drowning in.

And when they were alone, they behaved the way people do when they've had enough practice.

Being married to Rome was harder than dating him had ever been, and part of her had known for a while that she was holding on past the point where holding on made sense. But there was embarrassment woven into the staying — the quiet kind that doesn't announce itself, that just sits heavy in your chest and makes leaving feel like confirmation. She had chosen this man. She had believed in this marriage. She had stood in front of everyone and said so twice now. Walking away felt like handing every doubt she had ever silenced a reason to speak.

So she held onto that one tear.

And she chose to try again.

Looking back now, she understood something she couldn't see then. Sometimes people renew their vows because they believe in what they're saying. Because the marriage is worth the ceremony and the words are worth repeating. And sometimes they do it because something is already broken, and saying the words again is the only way left to pretend otherwise. She wasn't sure, standing in that hotel room, which one they were.

She wasn't sure she wanted to know.

Two months after the vow renewal, the loss came.

And during that time, Celeste and Rome were almost inseparable.

*Grief is not an excuse. Pain is not a permission slip.
And love was never meant to cost you your safety.*

— Sable Miles

TEN
The Breaking Point

For nearly two weeks the house stayed full — people, noise, smoke, someone always pouring something or rolling something or telling a story that was really just another way of not sitting with the silence.

One night after everyone had finally gone home, they sat outside in the yard and looked up at the sky. That was when he said it.

"Once all this is over… I just want to be near water."

He said it quietly, like a thought that slipped out before he meant to share it.

She remembered. Strangely, in the middle of all that grief, things between them felt lighter than they had in a long time. Not healed. Not whole. But something small had reignited — enough that she could feel it, enough that she held onto it carefully.

One morning during that week, the house went quiet for a moment. They were lying in bed when his phone rang.

FaceTime.

He answered without checking the screen. A woman appeared — smiling, an older woman seated beside her.

"Hey," she said. "You busy? Mommy wanted to talk to you."

Mommy?, But the woman didn't look familiar to Celeste.

They were both looking at him with the ease of people who had known him a long time. Rome shifted the phone and pulled Celeste into the frame.

"Lying here with my wife," he said.

The way he said it felt less like an introduction and more like a warning.

The woman's expression changed slightly.

"Oh," she said. "Okay. We were just checking on you."

The call ended. Celeste looked at him.

"Who was that?"

He barely glanced up.

"Just one of the girls from church."

She left it there. And added her to her memory bank.

The house stayed busy that entire week. People came through every night — family, old friends, exes. David came almost every evening. Kim stopped by a couple of times. Rome's cousin brought her best friend, Stacey, more than once. The living room stayed full and loud, smoke hanging in the air, liquor bottles lining the counter, music running later than it should. Grief didn't look like crying every night. It looked like distraction — people laughing too hard, stories repeating themselves, anything to keep the silence away.

Usually Celeste sat beside Rome with her glass of wine while he smoked and drank. But that week she joined in — drinking, smoking, sometimes edibles too. She told herself it was just to take the edge off. To carry the heaviness without breaking under it. She didn't think much about the antidepressants she'd been on since her recovery. She just needed to get through the week.

Rome stayed in the center of it all — drinking more than usual, moving from conversation to conversation, stepping outside sometimes and coming back in like nothing had shifted.

By the time the funeral came, the house felt drained. The noise had slowed. The crowd had thinned. Like everyone had finally remembered why they were there.

She sat beside Rome while he stared straight ahead, jaw tight, dark shades on, hand in hers. She squeezed and held on and tried to be whatever he needed her to be in that moment.

After the repast, people gathered again, and she was still trying.

By then she was ready to go. The noise and the constant energy had worn on her, and she moved through the room slowly, scanning faces — many of them unfamiliar, people who carried history with Rome that she was still learning the shape of.

That was when she noticed her. Across the room, the woman from the FaceTime call stood comfortably among Rome's relatives — moving easily between conversations, smiling, completely at home. Celeste watched her for a moment. Later she quietly asked one of Rome's cousins who she was.

He shrugged. "Oh, that's Erica. One of Rome's old girls. But she ain't nobody to worry about, cuz."

Casual. Dismissive. Like it didn't deserve another thought.

Then she spotted Brandi — talking and laughing with one of Rome's aunts like she had every right to be there. Which, by everyone else's understanding of the room, she did. Rome's past wasn't somewhere behind them. It was present, walking around, hugging people, refilling its cup.

Then Tyra walked in. She made an entrance like she wanted the room to feel her arrival. People greeted her warmly. At some point she stood and began telling stories — not the quiet kind people share at gatherings like this, but the kind that fills space and demands an audience. She talked about when she and Rome were young, how they met, how he hadn't always been a good boyfriend but had become a great man. That was why they would always be family.

Celeste was sitting at the opposite end of the same table.

Tyra's boyfriend sat beside her, eyes on his phone.

One of Rome's relatives looked directly at Celeste.

"Celeste… you okay?"

She nodded. Gave a small smile.

Inside, she was imagining flipping that entire table over. This was the second time Tyra had disrespected her — but this wasn't the time or the place.

Eventually, her eyes met Rome's across the room. He gave her a tired, warm smile — the kind that said he was grateful she was still standing. But the room had started pressing in on her, and she walked over and leaned close to him.

"Hubby, I'm ready to go."

He looked confused. "Now?"

"Yes."

"Why?"

"I have a headache."

He studied her face for a moment. Then nodded. They slipped out quietly before anyone could stop them. The air outside was cooler. The world was suddenly smaller and quieter, and she exhaled for what felt like the first time all day.

They got in the car without speaking. She was holding something carefully — the plan she had been sitting on for days. Neither of them mentioned the room full of women they had just left.

When she turned onto the highway instead of the road home, Rome looked over.

"Wifey, you're going the wrong way."

"Surprise, Hubby." She smiled. "We're headed to the ocean."

He blinked. "The ocean? Why?"

"Because you said you wanted to be near water."

He was quiet for a moment. "That was just something I said."

"And I remembered."

He nodded slowly. Then: "I don't even have nothing to wear."

"I packed days ago. Everything's in the trunk. Even your slippers."

He looked at her with an expression she couldn't quite read — somewhere between grateful and unsettled. She handed him a beer from the cooler and told him to relax. The rest of the drive stayed quiet. Not hostile. Just heavy in the way grief stays in the body even when no one is speaking.

The hotel room was clean and quiet, with a balcony opening toward the water. You could hear the waves from inside. For a moment, it felt like exactly what she had hoped for.

Rome dropped his bag and looked around.

"This is random," he said.

"It's not random."

"It feels random."

She exhaled. "I planned this when you said you wanted to be near water."

He stiffened. "My cousin set up a gathering tonight."

"I didn't know that when I booked this. I made these plans days ago."

His jaw tightened. "Sometimes you just move too fast."

"How is this moving too fast? We've been going nonstop for weeks."

"Nah." He shook his head. "This ain't about that. You pulled me away from my family because you're jealous."

"Of what?"

"Of everybody. Brandi. Tyra. Anybody that knew me before you."

"Rome, please."

"Yeah." His voice sharpened. "You're so damn insecure."

"I planned this because I wanted you to relax," she said. "Not because I'm insecure."

He laughed — not amused, just sharp — and stepped closer. She watched something shift behind his eyes. Not grief anymore. Something colder.

His finger came up in her face. Close enough that she leaned back. Something in his eyes had already gone somewhere she didn't recognize.

"You're so fucking jealous and insecure it's sickening."

"Ain't nobody jealous."

"Yes you are," he snapped. "You're a silly bitch."

"Rome, don't talk to me like that."

"I'll talk to you however I want. I'm so sick of you."

She didn't see it coming.

His hands found her throat before her mind had finished processing that he was moving toward her.

She remembered the weight of him — how much of him there was, how little of her. The force of it pushed her back onto the bed. His full weight above her. His face close. Something in his expression she had never seen before — grief and rage tangled into something darker than either one alone.

His hands tightened.

The room narrowed. Her vision blurred at the edges. She couldn't pull air in. She stopped fighting — not because she gave up, but because her body had nothing left to give. She went still. Tears ran down the sides of her face. She looked straight up into his eyes.

"You're doing this to me?" she said. Her voice was barely sound. "To me?"

Something moved across his face.

The pressure eased. His hands fell away. He stepped back, chest heaving, breathing like he had been the one struggling for air. The silence that followed was total.

They stared at each other across that small hotel room like two people who had just stepped somewhere neither of them could walk back from.

She got up.

She picked up her bags.

She walked out.

The hallway was too quiet after what had just happened inside that room. Her hands were shaking. Her neck burned where his hands had been. When she reached the car she sat without starting it, just breathing, staring at her reflection in the rearview mirror.

Her eyes looked different.

Not just angry. Alert. The kind of alert that arrives when your body finally understands what your heart has been refusing to.

She had planned this trip because she wanted to show up for her husband. Because she thought grief would make him easier to reach. Because she believed that if she loved him the right way, at the right moment, they would find their way back to each other.

But sitting in that car, she understood something she hadn't let herself understand before. The man in that hotel room hadn't looked like someone undone by grief. He looked like someone comfortable hurting her.

And for the first time since they had gotten married, the questions came — the ones she had never allowed herself to ask out loud, not even to herself.

Did this man even love her? Why did he marry her?

She sat with the engine off and the night quiet around her. Then she started the car. A few minutes later her phone rang. Rome. She didn't answer. Then a text came through.

Wifey, I need you. Please forgive me.

She stared at the message. Threw the phone into the passenger seat.

What kind of woman leaves her husband during a time like this?

She turned the car around.

When she got back to the room, Rome was standing at the door. He pulled her inside and held on, and they both cried — his arms around her, her face against his chest, tears that meant different things running together like they were the same.

He said he was overwhelmed. Said grief was doing something to him he didn't know how to control.

She didn't know if his tears were guilt or grief or something else entirely. Hers were exhaustion. And something she didn't have a name for yet.

The next morning, they had breakfast along the shoreline. The ocean was calm. They held hands.

On the drive home, he kept reaching for her like the night before had been a dream they had both agreed not to mention. She let him. She let him hold her hand.

She wasn't ready to say out loud what she already knew.

When they got home, things shifted quietly — the kind of shift you don't notice until you're already deep inside it. She slipped into routine. Sleep, work, home, repeat.

Rome fell asleep on the couch most nights. Sometimes she woke him. Sometimes she didn't. She was becoming less present as a wife. Less available. Not dramatically, not all at once — just gradually.

The way water recedes.

She was there.

But something in her had already left.

He was grieving his loss.

And she was grieving her marriage.

You weren't looking for trouble. You were looking for the truth. There's a difference — even when the truth is the most troubling thing you find.

— Sable Miles

ELEVEN
The Search

Celeste believed in trying everything before walking away. That was how she was raised and it was how she had moved through this marriage — one more attempt, one more conversation, one more chance. So she made an appointment with a marriage counselor. Counselor Owen. Rome didn't believe in sitting across from a stranger and unpacking his marriage — God was his counselor, he said. But she asked him to try and he showed up. Again. That counted for something.

Or so she thought.

Counselor Owen called her *Kelly* in their first session.

She let it go.

He called her *Lisa* in the second.

She looked at Rome.

Rome looked at the floor.

That silence told her more than any apology ever could.

Counselor Owen kept moving through his questions, his framework, his process — unbothered by the names leaving his mouth. Kelly. Lisa. Two women she had found in her husband's phone, now sitting in the mouth of the man they had hired to help them. Rome said nothing. Didn't correct him. Didn't even flinch. Just sat there, arms folded, letting another man call his wife by the wrong name while she sat three feet away.

She breathed through it and corrected Counselor Owen herself.

"I came here for help," she said, "and you're calling me the names of the women I'm here about."

He apologized and moved on. Rome never mentioned it. Not in the session. Not in the car. Not once. It was small, but it stayed with her. A pebble in her shoe she refused to remove.

What he did say, near the end of the hour, was this —

"What if I give up all my friends and the marriage still don't work out? What then? I'm supposed to go back and ask them to be my friends again?"

Counselor Owen nodded like the question deserved real consideration.

Celeste sat very still.

Her husband had just told a marriage counselor — in front of her, out loud, in a room they were paying for — that his friends were what he was protecting. Not the marriage. Not her. His circle.

The same circle that included women he had history with, women whose names were apparently close enough to the surface that a stranger could pull them out without even trying.

Rome said God was his counselor.

But God wasn't in that room.

Just her, Owen, and finally — the truth about where she ranked. The ride home was quiet. She watched the road. He offered nothing, and the silence between them learned a new shape. When they got home she went straight to the bedroom.

And that night, for the first time, she started looking with both eyes open. Not because she wanted to catch him — but because something in her finally stopped protecting the version of him she loved.

After that trip, nothing changed. She just stopped pretending it hadn't. The quiet between them got heavier. Rome started falling asleep in his man cave most nights.

Sometimes she would wake him and tell him to come to bed. Sometimes she didn't. She realized, slowly and then all at once, that she preferred the space.

The distance meant fewer conversations. Fewer opportunities for something ordinary to turn into something that wasn't. Her routine became simple: work, home, bedroom, sleep, repeat. From the outside, the house still functioned like a marriage. They spoke when they needed to. They moved around each other without much friction. They were civil in the particular way people are when something between them has broken and neither one is ready to say so.

A part of her had shut down.

Another part had woken up. The part that had been whispering for years, waiting for her to listen.

Rome would pass out, and she would start her search.

That's what it had become by then — methodical, quiet, almost practiced. She knew where to look and how long she had. The thing about searching is that eventually the phone stops feeling like evidence and starts feeling like a mirror. And mirrors don't lie — they just wait for you to stop looking away. They show you exactly what you've been arranging your life around not seeing.

She found something almost every time she looked.

Most of it she had already learned how to carry.

But this one stopped her.

She had to read it twice before her mind would accept what her eyes were already telling her.

Rome. And. Pam.

She set the phone down. Picked it up again. Set it back down.

Family. Again.

Blood had never guaranteed loyalty — she had learned that long before Rome. And she and Pam hadn't been close for years — not since Pam tried to get with a man Celeste had been with before Rome. She cut her off. Completely. Some lines, once crossed, don't get redrawn. And some people cross them with both feet like they were never there.

But before all that — before the distance and the cutoff — they had been family. Back then, Pam and Celeste were still on good terms when she first met Rome. She had shown Pam his profile picture when they first started talking — the way you do when something new and good is happening and you want to share it.

Pam had looked at it. Said something vague. Smiled.

But Celeste had caught something in her face before she composed it.

"What — you know him?"

"Nah," Pam said. "He's just cute."

She left it there. She had no reason not to. Pam was family.

She had unknowingly pointed her cousin right in his direction. And Pam had walked straight toward him without ever once looking back at her.

The messages weren't recent. That was the first thing she noticed — and somehow it made everything worse. These weren't from inside the marriage. They were from before it. From when she and Rome were still just dating.

She sat with the timestamps for a long time, running the math the way you do when your mind is trying to build a complete picture from pieces it keeps wanting to put down.

Pam hadn't been part of her life anymore. But she was still there. Moving through the background of Celeste's life, still trying to walk in her shoes.

The messages themselves were flirtatious. Playful. Familiar. Nothing explicit. Nothing that would read as significant to anyone who didn't know who was on either side of them. He didn't seem to know Pam. But Pam knew exactly who he was.

Pam was seeking to be messy. He was seeking attention. Two different hungers. Same outcome. Same wound. That difference had been clear. But the click didn't come until later — when Pam's words from their last phone argument came back to her.

"I could shatter your whole world."

She said it and hung up. No explanation. No context.

Just dropped it and left.

Celeste understood now what she had been holding. Secrets age, but they don't lose weight. And the timing didn't make it smaller. It made it heavier.

There are things that hurt because they're unexpected. And there are things that hurt because of what they mean. Because of who they involve. Because of what it says about the person you married.

And there was one name that kept appearing more than the others, determined to stay relevant by any means in a married man's life.

Erica.

At first, the messages weren't long — just small exchanges, comments, replies, reactions. The kind that look harmless on the surface. But the consistency made her pause.

Erica was using his loss as her reason to keep in contact. Once or twice a week like clockwork.

This was the same woman across the room talking comfortably with his relatives. The one his cousin had brushed off like she was nothing. Celeste stared at the screen — not because of anything specific in the messages. Just the presence. Erica's need to stay seen. Some women orbit a man long after he stops being their sun.

She picked up her phone. Typed Erica's name into the search bar. She already had a face. Rome's cousin had given her the name at the repast. What she didn't have yet was the full picture. And something about the ease of that FaceTime call — the way Erica had appeared on her husband's screen with her mother beside her like it was the most natural thing in the world — wouldn't let her leave it alone.

Among the five Ericas, her page wasn't hard to find. Public. Photos, church announcements, a life arranged carefully for other people to see. Celeste scrolled without knowing exactly what she was looking for. Just looking. Because sometimes the truth doesn't hide — it waits. It waits for you to stop lying to yourself.

Kelly still had her blocked. Brandi never accepted her friend request — she only wanted to be friends with Celeste's husband. But Erica's page was wide open. She checked her mutuals. And she almost dropped her glass of wine.

Renee.

You ain't gotta marry him, Renee. Her old culinary school friend who had laughed with her on the phone all those years ago, who had told her exactly who Rome was before she ever let him in.

She sat there staring at the screen. The connection was right there — small, quiet, completely unbothered by what it meant.

She called Renee.

Renee answered on the second ring, warm the way she always was.

"Celeste! What's good, girl?"

"Renee." Celeste kept her voice even and got straight to the point. "Who is this Erica chick that's on your page?"

A pause. Short but real.

"Girl, what Erica?"

Celeste gave the full name.

"Girl, that's one of my coworkers, she cool. Why? What's going on?"

"She's been in contact with my husband," Celeste said.

"Girl." Renee exhaled. "I heard you got married, but when I found out it was Rome, I nearly passed out. How? Why?" They both laughed. "When I seen y'all wedding pics, girl, I just shook my head and said this girl has got to be crazy."

"Girl, yes, dealing with this man," Celeste said.

"And he must don't know who he married to, out here still being Rome. He got the right one now. And my coworker — fake holy ass."

"Renee, tell her to stay out of my husband's inbox if she knows what's good for her."

"Girrrl, you know I am. She must don't know that he's married, the way she always preaching at work."

"She would have to be blind because our wedding pictures are on his page and his status reads married."

"I can't believe Erica is on that kind of time."

"Well believe it, she even had the nerve to FaceTime him with her momma while we were lying in bed."

"Girl, you lying!"

"I'm so sorry Celeste, sounds like Rome hasn't changed one bit, but I tried to warn you."

"Child, yes you did, woo!"

They stayed on the phone a little longer — not about Rome, just talking, the way old friends do when something heavy has just passed between them and neither one wants to end the call.

When she hung up she sat quietly in the dark.

Thinking about how small their town really was and how embarrassing it was to be married to Rome.

The church girl Rome had brushed off like she was nobody was her homegirl's coworker.

There had been a mutual connection this whole time.

She poured herself a tall glass of wine after that. But the search wasn't finished — she was hoping to come across these tens he used to date. No luck there.

She started sending things to her phone so she could examine them closer — without jumping every five minutes thinking Rome was going to wake up. Evidence feels different when you're saving it for yourself, not for a fight.

And then she saw it.

Stacey.

Yummy.

The first message was sent right around the time he moved in.

She looked back on his page. He posted a selfie that day.

Rome replied with a laughing emoji.

The second message stopped her.

It had been sent the morning of their wedding.

From Rome.

An inappropriate video — playful, sexual, the kind of message you send someone you've already crossed lines with.

Stacey had responded with a heart-eye emoji. That was it. Nothing more, but Celeste understood the context. Stacey had been at her wedding. She danced with her. Hugged her. Then sat in her home like she belonged there.

Laughing.

Like nothing required explanation.

Celeste grabbed her chest. It wasn't heartbreak — it was recognition. She screamed to herself because she couldn't wake him up. Couldn't let him know what she had just found. Couldn't give him the chance to explain it away before she had even finished reading it.

She sat there with her wine and went back and forth with herself. None of this was new information exactly — Stacey had been a year ago. Pam even further back than that. Old enough to argue away. Old enough for Rome to say that was before, that was different, that was then. And part of her already knew he would. Part of her was already constructing his defense before he even opened his mouth.

So she sat with it. Silence had become her safest place to fall apart.

She felt foolish bringing it up.

She felt more foolish not to.

So she held it the way she had learned to hold things — quietly, carefully, turning it over in the dark until she understood what she was actually going to do with it.

She didn't say anything to Rome.

Not that night.

Not the next day.

Instead, she started noticing more.

Patterns.

Times.

Names.

And the more she looked, the more something settled into place. None of it felt shocking anymore. It felt familiar. Like something she had known long before she ever opened his accounts. Something she ignored because she wanted the marriage to work.

Because she believed commitment meant pushing doubt aside.

Because she told herself trust was supposed to feel like patience. But now patience looked a lot like silence. And silence had started giving other people access to her life.

So she kept watching.

Not to catch him.

To understand.

Because understanding hurts less than being blindsided.

The marriage she was actually in. Not the one she kept defending. Not the one she kept resuscitating. Not the one she thought she had.

Because the truth was getting harder to ignore.

And if she kept looking long enough —

She would see it clearly.

She let it settle into the place where she kept everything else she had learned to carry quietly.

And she understood something with a clarity that felt cold.

The marriage she was trying to protect had edges she hadn't fully mapped yet.

There were still things she didn't know.

And not knowing them wouldn't protect her.

So she kept digging. Not out of curiosity — out of survival.

Blood can't be trusted. Real or fake. Loyalty had never been her family's strong suit.

So she confronted him. She didn't remember choosing the moment — it arrived the way those moments always do, in the middle of something ordinary.

He was on the couch.

She was standing in the doorway.

"I know about Pam."

He went still.

"Who?"

"Don't do that," she said. "I read it. I know."

A pause.

Then —

"Celeste — who? What are you talking about?"

"Oh now you don't know who she is?"

"Are you serious right now? I told you. I don't even know that girl."

"That's not what her messages said."

He exhaled, frustrated. Just taking it all in.

"Then you gonna go mess around with my homegirl's coworker! Rome, I went to school with that girl, how fucking embarrassing."

"Wifey, you are driving me crazy with all this." He grabbed his head and pushed it back. "Who is your homegirl coworker?"

"Erica, you know your ex, from church."

What followed wasn't an explanation.

It was a negotiation.

The kind where the goal isn't truth — it's the version of the story that costs him the least.

He minimized.

Redirected.

Brought up things she had done.

Things she had said.

Ways she had failed him too.

Because when you can't defend yourself, you distribute the weight.

She sat through all of it.

She didn't yell.

Didn't cry.

By then her feelings didn't arrive loudly.

They arrived quietly.

Then she hit him with Stacey.

"And what about you and Stacey on our wedding day?"

She pulled out her phone.

Showed him the messages.

Date circled.

"On our wedding day, Rome. You been making me look stupid from the very beginning. This was all one big joke."

"Stacey — you questioning me about Stacey's dirty ass? She messed with me and my homeboys back in the day. So what?"

"So what? So what you had that bitch at my wedding?"

"What?" He shook his head. "Wifey, that girl is not thinking about me."

"Maybe not now," she said. "But she was. The day of our wedding."

Her voice broke.

"She danced with me."

"And she sat in my home, knowing she had fucked my husband."

"Because we just friends, that girl like—"

"Don't you dare say it, Rome. Don't you dare say it."

"She family. That girl is like—"

"I said don't."

He said it anyway.

"She like family, Wifey."

She looked at him.

"I can't do this no more," he said. "You driving me crazy. Celeste, no man in their right mind would put up with all your detective shit."

The room went quiet in a different way after that. He started gathering his things. Not slow. Fast. Like a man who had already decided.

Part of her felt relief.

The other part felt the floor shift.

She didn't beg. Didn't cry. Didn't ask him to stay.

"If you walk out that door," she said, "don't come back."

Then she went to the bathroom, turned the shower on as hot as it would go, and stood under it until all she could feel was the water.

The decision was his now. Not hers.

When a person shows you who they are in private, believe them. When they show you in the street — that's God making sure you don't have an excuse anymore.

— Sable Miles

TWELVE

In the Streets

Rome made his choice — just not the one Celeste expected. After her shower she checked his location. Still home. She walked down to the man cave and there he was, passed out drunk on the couch she had customized for him. All that noise, all that chaos, and for a moment after the argument, the house was quiet enough to almost feel like peace.

The first time she saw Stacey after finding the message, it wasn't planned.

It happened at one of Wendy's family gatherings — one of those casual ones where everyone shows up, food everywhere, music low, kids running through the house, people talking over each other in loose circles. Celeste almost didn't go. Rome's world meant Wendy's family, which meant David, which meant Kim — and Kim was the kind of woman who threw shade and then looked genuinely confused when you reacted. *Ain't nobody going to steal your husband, Celeste.* She had said that once, smiling, surrounded by people. Celeste had learned to play along for the sake of their husbands' friendship.

Staying home felt like surrender.

So she went.

Rome moved through the room the way he always did — comfortable, easy, completely at home. This was his world. His people. Celeste stayed near the edges at first, speaking when spoken to, smiling when expected, trying to keep the noise in her head from showing on her face.

Then she saw her.

Stacey.

Standing near the kitchen, laughing, moving through the room like she belonged there. Which, by everyone else's understanding of the room, she did. Nobody in that house knew what Celeste knew. Nobody had any reason to look at Stacey the way Celeste was looking at her now.

She watched her for a moment before Stacey saw her. Celeste tried to understand how this woman moved through her world so freely and disrespectfully. How she could have danced at Celeste's wedding — actually danced with her — and sat in her home like nothing required explanation. Like whatever she and Rome had exchanged that morning was just a small thing, something that didn't require her to move differently around his wife.

Stacey spotted her before Celeste could decide what to do with her face.

"Celeste!"

She walked toward her the way she always had — open, warm, arms already reaching.

Celeste didn't move.

She let Stacey get close enough to believe the hug was coming. Then she stepped back. Stacey's arms hung briefly in the air before she lowered them. Celeste touched her arm lightly, just enough to guide her a few steps to the side, away from the center of the room. Her voice stayed quiet. Calm.

"Don't touch me."

It was the first time Celeste let her feel the boundary she'd crossed long before Celeste ever named it. Stacey's expression shifted — not defensive, just confused. Like she was replaying their last interaction, trying to find the moment that explained this.

"I'm sorry you feel that way," Stacey said.

She didn't know that Celeste knew. And Celeste wasn't going to explain it here, in the middle of his family's house, with people two feet away. This wasn't that moment. This was just Celeste finally drawing a line that should have existed a long time ago.

She walked away before Stacey could say anything else.

Clear. Direct. Final.

Not every confrontation needed to be loud to be real.

Kim arrived shortly after. They were cordial. Nothing more.

Celeste told Rome she was ready to leave not long after the Stacey moment. He looked surprised but didn't push back. They said their goodbyes and walked out. David had just pulled up as they were leaving, and Rome stopped at the curb to talk to him while Celeste walked ahead to the car. They were parked on a quiet side street, the sound of the gathering muffled from there. She slid into the passenger seat and closed her eyes. Her temples were throbbing.

When Rome got in, he started the engine and turned the music up.

Loud.

"Can you turn that down? I have a headache."

He glanced at her. "Why? What's wrong with you?"

"My head hurts. I just need a minute."

But Rome never heard pain unless it was his.

He looked at her sideways.

"I know you not tripping over Stacey."

It wasn't just Stacey. It was everything stacked underneath her — the wedding-morning message, the dancing, the nights in their living room, the ease of it all. It was the gathering and the women and the way Rome's world was always full of this, always, like it couldn't exist any other way. And it was the part of her that had been carrying this for so long she couldn't tell where the weight ended and she began.

It was all too much.

Rome lit a cigarette. Exhaled. Then turned to her and said it plainly.

"You one silly bitch."

Celeste turned slowly toward him.

"I know you didn't just call me a bitch."

He laughed. Low. Unbothered.

"You really letting a bum-ass bitch like Stacey get under your skin?" He shook his head. "You's a stupid bitch."

"Rome. Don't call me out my name."

"Or what, bitch?"

He dragged the last word out like he enjoyed it.

Something in her snapped. There's a point where disrespect stops being shocking and starts being familiar — and that's the point that breaks you.

She popped him in the mouth before she finished deciding to.

His head jerked back. For a moment they just stared at each other. The music still playing. The street still quiet outside the windows.

Then he smiled.

Not amused.

Mean.

"Bitch, hit me again."

So she did.

His fist came back faster than she could brace for. The punch landed and her face went hot — not pain at first, just heat, then the pain right behind it. Adrenaline took over before fear could.

There was a cooler on the floor from the gathering. She grabbed it and swung. He kept hitting her. The car felt like it was shrinking.

At some point she was between the seats and his hands were around her throat again — the same hands, the same pressure, the same hotel room narrowing in her memory, overlapping with right now.

At some point the door flew open.

Celeste was suddenly outside the car, on the ground. She didn't remember how she got there. She was looking up at the night sky and then at the underside of her husband's laced-up boot — the tread of it hovering inches from her face, close enough that she could see the dirt pressed into the grooves.

David and Kim were shouting from across the street.

"Come on, y'all!"

They ran toward them. Kim reached Celeste first, pulling her up, holding her back. David grabbed Rome. Kim had always been shady, but she showed up in that moment, and Celeste couldn't decide whether it was genuine or just Kim making sure she had a story to tell later.

Rome was bleeding from his hand. She had bitten him somewhere in the chaos of it.

"You lucky I didn't stomp your ass to death out here!" He was still trying to get around David. "You bitch! That nothing-ass bitch — you really tried to bite my hand off!"

"You tried to hurt me!" Celeste was still pulling against Kim's grip. "I'm your wife!"

"I'm your husband, you nasty-mouth bitch! Who bites their husband?"

"Me." She didn't look away. "So you can remember to keep your hands to yourself, fuck boy! Fuck you, Rome!"

The street was quiet except for their voices, and the gathering was just around the corner, and somewhere in that house, his family was sitting with food and music and no idea that his wife was on the ground outside looking up at the bottom of his boot.

The adrenaline drained slowly. Her face hurt. Her neck hurt. Her hands were trembling. She could still feel the moment she realized how far things had gone — and how far they could have gone if no one had intervened.

And she kept thinking the same thing on a loop, quieter each time, like something settling rather than rising:

This wasn't a marriage anymore. This was a man who had stopped seeing her as someone he loved. This was a man who could hurt her in the street and feel justified.

This was the moment her body understood what her heart had been refusing to.

*I tried to leave but I kept coming
back to the warmth of you.*

— Warsan Shire

THIRTEEN

The Reconciliation

The morning after, Celeste checked Rome's accounts before she even got out of bed. Rome had reached out to Kelly — Ms. Lunch Date herself. She had him blocked, so he went through their mutual friends instead, desperate enough to go the long way around. Neither one of them responded. Not even two hours after his wife had been on the ground outside a car, and he was already back to being Rome.

Rome never came back to the house after that night. Not to stay, not even to visit. David had taken him in, and sometime after that Rome got his own place. He refused to help with any of the bills. So Celeste switched everything back over to her name and cut his phone off. Not smart — but she wanted peace of mind more than leverage. It felt like taking something back.

Time passed after the fight. The kind of time where the anger cools but the damage stays — not days, but months. Two, to be exact.

For a while they didn't speak at all. Eventually he reached out again after he got a new line — but only when something practical needed handling. Mail. Paperwork. The small administrative threads that keep two lives connected whether the people in them want to be or not.

Other than that, he made it clear she was no longer his responsibility. She told herself she was fine with that. One thing she knew how to do was survive.

And she did. For a while.

But surviving and living are two different things. The house was quiet in a way that had stopped feeling like peace and started feeling like absence. Not his absence specifically — she had made her peace with that. Just the particular emptiness of a life built around another person that hadn't yet figured out what it was without them.

And then one night she called, and he answered. She wouldn't dress it up. At this point she was single too — but why see someone else's husband when she could see her own.

They started seeing each other again before they ever sat down and talked about anything. No conversation first, no resolution, no agreement about what had gone wrong or what would be different. Just two people who knew each other well enough to fall back into something familiar when the silence got too heavy. It wasn't reconciliation. It wasn't forgiveness. It was something more complicated than either — the particular gravity of a person you've chosen, even when the choosing has cost you more than you planned to spend.

The first time she went to his place, she walked in and did what she always did in a new space — moved her eyes across the room, taking inventory.

And there they were. Sitting on top of the media console. Right out in the open, not tucked away, not turned around. Two pottery plates — the kind you make at a ceramic studio. Fired, glazed, finished. Each one engraved with initials. One read *Forever Mines.* The other, blue and white, his team colors.

She picked it up slowly. It was the kind of evidence that didn't need explanation — it spoke in a language she already understood.

"It's been two months and you're already in a relationship?"

"Celeste, what are you talking about?"

He was already drinking by the time she got there.

"Nothing apparently," she said, and set it back down.

She didn't make a scene. Didn't push. She noted it the way she had trained herself to note things by then — quietly, without letting him see it land. But it did. Because the fact that he would leave those plates sitting in plain sight, knowing she was coming over, wasn't carelessness.

Or maybe it was.

Either way, it said something. A man who wanted his wife back would have thought about those plates before she walked through the door. A man who hadn't quite decided would leave them exactly where they were and see what happened.

He hadn't decided.

And she stood there holding that plate like a woman who already knew exactly why she came — and still felt it land. Two months of silence. Two months of surviving the wreckage of what he had done to her — to them — and those plates were right there. In plain sight. Not tucked away. Not turned around. Out. Like he wanted her to see them. Like he needed her to know there was someone else.

That was what landed hardest. Not the plates themselves. The possibility that he had left them exactly where they were on purpose. And that she had walked in and given him exactly what he wanted anyway.

She filed it away and kept moving.

He reached for her when she got up to leave. She never had plans to stay. Especially once she saw he was really out here dating — seemingly in a relationship. She was still honoring a marriage he had already walked out of. But he was the last one she ever planned to love. So she took what she needed and left. She was being careful while he was still being reckless.

The second time she came over was about a week later, and the plates were still there. She had already done her research, so she knew exactly who the woman was. The church girl herself — Renee's coworker, Erica. Celeste wanted to throw those plates and him into the fireplace, but she stayed focused on the mission at hand. She wasn't there for Erica. She was there for herself.

But looking at those plates and thinking about how disrespectful her husband was left her feeling foolish. Now she felt like a mistress in her own marriage. There's a special kind of humiliation in realizing you're competing in a race you never agreed to run in. She knew then this would be the last time she ever crossed that threshold.

Learning how to truly be with herself would be difficult. But it was better than anything that had to do with this man.

But Rome had other plans. That night he wanted to talk. So they finally talked — not the surface-level, practical kind of talking they had been doing. Real talking. The kind that requires something from you. At some point Rome went quiet in the way he did when something was sitting heavy.

Then he said it.

"I miss my wife."

He had been drinking, so she wasn't sure if it was him talking or the liquor. So she just listened.

Rome said he had been doing a lot of thinking and wanted his marriage back.

"I know I messed up and I'm sorry, Wifey."

There it was. *Wifey.* Honestly, that word softened her right up.

She sat there and listened and tried to measure how much of what he was saying she believed, and how much she simply wanted to believe, and how blurry the line between those two things had gotten over the years.

"So you want your wife back but have another woman on display?"

"Come on now, Wifey — a woman on display? What you talking about?"

She pointed to the plates.

"That ain't nothing. That girl don't mean nothing to me. This was just some chick I was seeing."

"Just some chick? You mean your ex? Your ex and my homegirl's coworker. The one who has a sweater in the closet, eyeliner on your dresser, and lip gloss in the nightstand."

"I didn't know she left all of that."

"Oh, but now you know who I'm talking about?"

"Celeste, Wifey, I'm a man with needs and I thought we were done."

"You thought we were done so you went and jumped in another relationship two months later, with my homegirl's coworker."

"Ain't nobody in a relationship."

"I can't tell."

Erica had left little telltale crumbs — the way women do when they're trying to mark territory, when they want to make their presence known to whoever comes next. It was the oldest trick in the book. One Celeste knew all too well. But she had left her mark on her husband a long time ago. She was always present, even when she wasn't.

"Wifey, please, I don't want to fight, I'm trying to fix us."

She rolled her eyes. "Rome, you so embarrassing."

He was lying. On top of the disrespect. And she was ready to go.

But he was still the last man she had ever planned to love, ever planned to be with. She hadn't wanted the marriage to end. She had wanted a better husband. And somewhere underneath all the damage — the fights, the names, the hotel room, the women, the years of it — she still believed that man existed somewhere inside the one she had been living with.

So she gave them a chance. Forgiveness had nothing to do with it. He was it, her one and only *'til death do them part. Right?*

Because somewhere in the part of her that still knew how to hope, she believed that what they had been at their best was real — and real things don't just disappear. They get buried. They get neglected. They get covered over by years of small betrayals and loud arguments and quiet accommodations. But they don't disappear. She had loved this man completely. She had given him things she had never given anyone. And she wasn't ready to accept that all of it had been for nothing.

The plates came down the next day. Not because he removed them. He never touched them. She threw them away herself, without explanation. He never asked about them. They never discussed it. They were simply gone one day, and they both stepped around the absence like they had never been there at all.

For a while things felt different. Not perfect — they were too far past perfect for that — but intentional. They moved around each other carefully. Gently, almost. Like two people relearning how to share space without breaking something. They went on dates. Stayed in. Cooked sometimes. Moved through the ordinary rhythms of a couple trying to rebuild, slowly closing the distance the separation had left between them.

She wasn't tracking him. Wasn't searching. Wasn't waiting for something to surface. She had made a decision to try and she was honoring it — fully, the way she had always believed commitment deserved to be honored. For the first time in a long time, she let herself stop anticipating the next thing.

She told herself the Erica chapter was closed. No notifications at odd hours. No familiar name glowing on the screen while she was lying beside him. No patterns she could feel building under the surface. She told herself that whatever had been happening before the separation had ended with it.

She wanted that to be true.

She chose to believe it.

Then he started leaving at the same time every morning.

It was subtle at first. Early enough that she could explain it away — he had mentioned something about adjusting his work schedule and getting into a new routine. That was reasonable. She accepted it. Left it alone.

But something in her had already been trained.

And this was a pattern.

Rome's favorite show was *Cheaters*. He had watched it beside her like a man with nothing to hide, smirking at the screen, narrating other people's downfall. She had taken notes.

The tracker had been on his car for a few days. There was one location that was familiar to her — not his job, not the casino, not anywhere he had ever mentioned. Just a spot near one of his favorite food places that he had no good reason to visit consistently because it was so far from where they lived or the area he covered. She had clocked it twice during the marriage and filed it both times.

Now here it was again during the reconciliation, like clockwork.

The pattern she noticed first wasn't even from the tracker. It was the FaceTime calls. Every time the dot landed on that location, she would call him. He never answered. But he always called back — always from the car, always moving, always sounding like he had just gotten off another line. Every time. Like clockwork. Her husband apparently had a lot of important calls happening near the same food spot an hour away.

She drove out there once. Sat and waited. Watched the street. Nothing came of it. An hour away, and she still couldn't find what she was looking for because the tracker wasn't as precise as the app on his phone.

He changed all the codes.

When she brought it up he didn't deny or deflect the way he usually did. He begged her. Quietly, seriously, with something behind his eyes she hadn't seen before.

Leave it alone, Wifey. Please.

That scared her for a minute.

That also told her everything the tracker couldn't.

She never found out who it was. By his reaction, she was almost afraid to.

She sat with it the way she had learned to sit with things — letting the information settle, waiting until she understood it fully before deciding what to do. And in the interim, she just kept showing up. Kept trying. Kept choosing the marriage she had said she was going to choose.

And every morning she chose it again. Not once — every single morning. Because choosing it once wasn't enough. The decision didn't hold overnight. It had to be remade in the dark before she opened her eyes, before she reached for her phone, before the day gave her another reason to question it. That was what nobody talks about when they talk about fighting for a marriage. It isn't one decision. It's the same decision, over and over, in the quiet before the world starts, when you are most honest with yourself and most tired and most aware of everything it is costing you.

She made that decision every morning. And every morning she got up and honored it. Even when she already knew what she knew.

Even when the knowing sat heavy on her chest before she'd even had coffee. She kept choosing. Because she had said she would. Because she still believed, in the part of her that hadn't yet learned better, that choosing hard enough and long enough would eventually be enough.

Rome wasn't just her husband. He was her last. And what bound them together went deeper than vows — deeper than anything she could have explained to anyone who hadn't been there when it began.

Because the truth — the part she wouldn't fully understand until later — was that she had walked back into the picture during a time when Rome was already somewhere else entirely. Already building something with Erica that had its own shape, its own rhythm, its own quiet consistency. She didn't know that yet. All she knew was what he had said that night, sitting across from her in his house.

I miss my wife.

And she had chosen to believe him.

She hadn't put it on him to catch him.

She had put it on him because she already knew.

And knowing, at that point, was the only thing she still had that was entirely hers.

The night before the pastor session, they sat together on the couch. Rome was drinking. She was nursing a glass of wine. They had been talking about nothing — the kind of evening conversation two people have when they're trying to practice being comfortable around each other again. She said something about the meeting. About going in together. About being ready for the next part.

Rome looked at her.

"Next part of what?"

She waited for him to laugh. He didn't. He was looking at her the way he looked at everything he didn't want to be held responsible for — blankly, patiently, like she was the one bringing something into the room that didn't belong there.

"Rome, you asked me to come back. You said you missed me. We've been trying for months."

He nodded slowly. "Yeah. I mean, I said that. But I don't know. I thought we was just hanging out. Seeing where it went."

Something quiet went through her chest, and she recognized it before it named itself. This was him. This was what he did. The declare. The retreat. The careful rewriting of what had been said so that whatever he did next couldn't be called a betrayal because there was nothing formal to betray. She had watched him do this for years. But she hadn't seen this monster in a while — not since the very beginning of them dating. Whenever he wanted to cheat in peace he would get amnesia about his commitment to her. He would conveniently forget telling her they were together, in a relationship — sometimes a week into it, sometimes three days after he'd told her he needed her and claimed her as his woman at his convenience. She thought he had grown out of that. But here they were again. Now married. Playing the same game.

Apparently not.

She didn't argue with him. She didn't explain. She didn't remind him of the night he'd said *I miss my wife* across his living room with real tears in his eyes. She just sat there with her wine and filed it, the way she had filed everything else, and waited for him to finish whatever he was building toward tomorrow.

Because this time, it wasn't an accident. He was clearing the runway.

That same night, after he fell asleep, she took the tracker off his car. Not because she believed in the fresh start anymore. Because she knew he would look for it tomorrow, and she wanted him to find nothing. She didn't want to give him anything he could point to when he decided to end it.

She walked into that room pretending to carry hope — because she wanted the pastor to see her try, even though she already knew. And once she mentioned the tracker in the session, she knew Rome would go looking for it afterward. Let him. It was already gone.

So they sat in his office across from each other like two people who still believed there was something left to repair. The room was quiet. Soft light came through the window. Books lined the shelves behind him.

Rome spoke first. He talked about misunderstandings, about pressure, about feeling like everything he did was wrong. He said that Celeste had changed and wasn't fun to be around anymore. The pastor listened and nodded. Then he turned to Celeste.

"And Celeste," he said gently, "sometimes men make mistakes. Sometimes people step outside of their marriage without fully understanding the damage it can cause."

Step outside. The phrase caught her attention. It was the kind of language men used to soften the blow they never had to feel. The way he said it made betrayal sound like a wrong turn — something accidental, something correctable. Something that could be softened with the right language.

She sat and listened while they talked about forgiveness. About grace. About the patience that marriages require. At one point tears gathered in her eyes.

The meeting with the pastor was supposed to help. But sitting across from Reverend Wells, she mentioned one of the locations — the one near a local hospital — and let that land without saying more.

"And see this another thing — she still in my phone. Tracking me like I'm a dog or something, I'm her husband! No man in their right mind would deal with this, Rev. No man!" He shook his head and gripped his fingers together tightly in his lap.

Then Celeste released all that had been filed away.

"When men cheat," she said, her voice uneven, "do they ever stop and think about what that does to their woman?"

The pastor waited.

She kept going.

"It's not just the betrayal." The tears came before she could stop them.

She stopped. Then started again.

"Men say the vision of their woman with another man is unshakable. Yet my husband expects me to shake off not one, not two, not even three women. Am I enough? Was I ever enough? Did you ever really love me? The torture is the same for us — so why are women expected to just get over it?"

She didn't finish.

She didn't have to.

The room already knew.

The pastor leaned forward. "Pain is part of the process," he said. "Healing requires understanding." He paused. "But from everything I've heard in this room today — you two just aren't compatible. Maybe you should see other people until you figure it out."

She stared at him, certain she had misheard. A pastor. Encouraging married people to date other people. She thought she was hearing things.

The tears came — a mixture of everything. He passed her a tissue. She turned to him and said firmly:

"I came here to save my marriage. Not for it to end."

He turned to Rome and said quietly, "Go comfort your wife."

Rome shifted in his seat. Started to move toward her.

"Don't," she said.

He stopped.

"Another man shouldn't have to tell you to console your wife."

Rome sat back. Something moved across his face — not guilt, not grief. Frustration. He threw his hands up slowly, the gesture of a man who had already decided what he was about to say.

"I can't do this anymore," he said. "Nothing I do is ever right." He shook his head. "I'm done—."

And he walked out.

The pastor studied her for a long moment after the door closed.

"You're one sharp cookie," he said finally. "You know exactly what you're talking about."

She looked him straight in his eyes.

"I know," she said. "But it doesn't make me feel any better."

She stayed behind for a moment, letting the room go quiet around her, then walked out and drove to Rome's place to collect the rest of her things. She called first. No answer. Sent a text. Nothing. When she pulled up, her things were scattered across the front lawn. Not much — a pair of sneakers, a jacket, her overnight bag. All of it tossed into the grass like it had been waiting for exactly this occasion. Rome stood in the doorway smoking a cigarette, like he'd been rehearsing this moment.

Celeste stared at the lawn for a long second, caught somewhere between disbelief and something close to dark amusement.

Then she laughed.

"Oh," she said, shaking her head. "You've been waiting your whole life to do this."

He shrugged. "Now you know how it feels."

She stepped forward to gather her things. Rome lifted his hands slightly.

"Go ahead, Celeste. I'm not trying to put my hands on you."

Before she could finish collecting her things, a police car pulled up. Then another.

"You called the police?" she asked.

"Yeah," he said calmly. "I don't want no problems."

"Rome," she said, bending to pick up her bag, "this is all you."

The officers asked for her ID, asked a few questions, then politely walked her back to her car. Rome finished his cigarette in the doorway and went inside before she had even pulled away.

She sat there with the engine running and her things in the passenger seat.

This man had thrown her belongings into the yard and called the police — on her, his wife — as though she were the disruption. As though none of it had started with him.

The decision had been made twice in one day. Once in the pastor's office. Once on this front lawn. She was done fighting for something that was never going to be what she needed it to be.

Later that evening, when Rome sent that text, she would have gone. Not to fight. Just to let him see her face so he'd know exactly how close she had been the whole time.

Her phone buzzed. One text from Rome.

Track me now bitch I'm on my way to my new bitch house. Come up there so she can beat your ass, bitch.

Her husband. Directing her to another woman's house. Inviting violence. One last humiliation on the way out the door.

She took a screenshot. Posted it to his social media page. Blocked him.

Then she sat there in the quiet, thinking about the few moments of happiness they had shared. About how two people can want the same thing and still destroy it.

They never stood a chance against each other. Not with the way he loved himself. And the way she loved him.

*What God joins together, let no man interfere with.
But sometimes the interference was already
standing at the altar.*

— Sable Miles

FOURTEEN
The Marriage She Mourned

Life kept moving. Bills still had to be paid. Work still expected her there. The world didn't pause just because hers had collapsed. Celeste moved through it on autopilot most days — wake, work, come home, sleep, repeat. When people asked how she was doing, she said *okay*. It was easier than explaining that *okay* didn't mean okay. It just meant she was still functioning.

Then one night she was scrolling and she saw it.

A photo.

Rome sitting at a long table in a ceramic studio, clay on his hands, a half-finished plate in front of him. Across the table sat Erica — clay on her hands too, her own plate in front of her, both of them smiling. Not the polite kind of smile people arrange for pictures. The relaxed kind. The kind that comes from a night that has already been good before anyone thinks to take a photo.

She looked at the date.

It was three days before she reached out to her husband for a physical reconciliation. Three days before she walked back into his life. Her husband had been sitting across from another woman, making something.

She zoomed in. Not because she needed proof — she had passed the point where proof changed anything. She zoomed in the way you do when your brain needs a moment to accept what your eyes already understand. They looked easy together. Natural. Like the space between them made sense. Like the years of her marriage had simply been something he outgrew while she was still trying to grow into it.

She put the phone down. Picked it up again. Put it down.

She sat with it for a long time that night — the particular stillness of a woman who has finally seen the thing she already knew. No tears. No rage. Just the quiet arrival of something that had been on its way for a long time and had finally found the door.

What hurt most wasn't the clay. Not the picture itself.

It was the ease.

The quiet, comfortable ease of it.

Some endings don't happen in a single moment. They happen in layers. And sometimes you don't realize the marriage is over until you see your husband smiling in a life that doesn't include you.

The first stretch, she kept herself moving — work, errands, plans, people. Staying busy is its own kind of medication. You fill every hour so the quiet can't find you. It worked for a while.

Then she sat still.

And the moment she sat still, everything she had been outrunning caught up with her at once. She stopped returning calls. Stopped making plans. Some mornings she made it as far as the couch and decided that was enough. Her therapist called it the crash that follows survival mode.

Months passed before she learned the full shape of it. Rome was back with one of his exes — and it wasn't Brandi.

She would be honest. Kelly, she expected. Brandi never wanted Rome the way she wanted the hold she had on him — that power, that access, that ability to pull the string whenever she felt like it. But Erica? She never saw her coming. Erica had been quiet about it. Patient. Sliding in and out of the background the whole time, using his grief as her in, showing up at family gatherings like she belonged there, leaving little crumbs around his house like she had been waiting for Celeste to clear out.

Or waiting her turn.

Erica didn't slide in. She slithered — slow and deliberate, back into the spot she had decided was hers all along. Some women don't steal — they pray over the door they're waiting to walk through. And life has a way of circling back on women who interfere where they were never invited.

That part hurt in a specific way. Not because Celeste wanted him. Because she had been watching the wrong woman the whole time.

During that time she found herself returning to the early years — the good parts, and there had been good parts. People don't stay in something for years without believing in it at some point. But with distance, the picture sharpened. She had spent years trying to hold together something that was already coming apart at the seams. And in the process, she had started coming apart too.

Then fate put Erica directly in her path.

She was at a sandwich shop when she saw her near the counter. For a moment she considered walking by, but she walked toward her instead.

"Well, if it isn't little Miss Church Girl."

Erica looked confused for a second, then smiled and opened her arms like they were old friends reconnecting.

Celeste gave her a look that stopped her cold.

Erica lowered her arms.

"This isn't about Rome," Celeste continued. "You can keep him. This is about me. You disrespected me. And there's a price to pay for that."

Erica raised an eyebrow. "And who are you?"

Celeste answered loud enough for the whole store to hear.

"I'm his wife!"

The store stopped. Someone near the counter whispered "oh my God." The air shifted the way it does when a truth lands somewhere public and there's nowhere to hide from it.

She said it with her whole chest. Never mind that her husband was probably somewhere across town with one of the others while she was standing here. She wasn't defending a marriage — she was defending the part of herself they treated like entertainment. The marriage was already gone. This was about her. Every single one of them — Rome included — had moved through her life like she wasn't a person worth considering.

She was tired of being treated like she didn't matter in her own story.

So yes. She said it with her whole chest. And it sounded better than it felt.

Erica looked at her for a long moment. Then she said the sentence she had clearly been saving.

"I know your husband better than you. You was stupid for marrying him."

Celeste felt something that was almost a laugh move through her chest and dissolve before it reached her face.

"So what does that make you?" she asked.

Erica didn't answer.

She turned and walked toward the door.

"You're going to need that hug before this is over," Celeste said calmly. "Won't He do it!"

Erica walked out without looking back.

The store folded back into its ordinary self around her — someone ordering at the counter, someone laughing near the door, the world continuing without any awareness of what had just happened inside it.

Celeste didn't move.

She ordered her food.

She had no reason to rush.

Erica was the one who had to leave.

When she got to the car she sat there for a long moment, engine off, food in her lap. And then she started laughing. Because she had just walked up to that woman and announced herself like she was still somebody's wife. *His* wife. She had said it with everything she had.

You really said his wife, Celeste.

She was so annoyed at herself she could barely stand it. Grief will make you perform roles you no longer believe in.

She reached into her bag and pulled out a cigarette. Lit it. Took a long drag and watched the smoke curl toward the windshield.

Somewhere along the way she had picked up Rome's habit. Of all the things that man had left behind, that was the one that followed her out.

She almost laughed again. Almost.

She never saw either of them in person again after that.

For a while, she checked their social media.

Not out of longing. Not out of hope. Out of something rawer — the compulsion that comes when you're waiting for the moment someone else finally sees what you already know. She needed to witness it. Needed to watch what disrespecting her would cost them.

Their pages told her everything she needed to know. Careful posts. Coded language. Scripture wrapped around things that had nothing to do with God. New relationship energy that nobody wanted to name out loud because naming it meant owning it. They all had reputations to protect. Versions of themselves to maintain.

So they coded it.

And she decoded every single one.

One of them posted a photo from a trip — just a hand in the frame, careful enough to hide a face but not careful enough to hide everything. She recognized that hand. She had held it at the altar. She had watched it reach for her in the dark. She knew every ring, every knuckle.

She wasn't surprised. Rome didn't belong to anyone. That had always been his rule — she had just spent years trying to be the exception.

She kept scrolling anyway. She told herself she was gathering information. Staying informed. That there was a practical reason to know what these women were doing, where they were posting, how they were framing what they had been a part of. She constructed very sensible explanations for why she was still watching.

None of them were true.

The truth lived in the specific feeling of picking up the phone. The way her thumb moved before her mind caught up. The way the brightness of the screen in a dark room had become familiar — almost comforting — even when what it showed her wasn't. She had a whole ritual by then and hadn't even noticed it forming. She wasn't checking on them — she was checking on the version of herself she had become.

Phone face down on the nightstand. Wait until the room was quiet. Pick it up like she was checking the time. Tell herself she was just looking.

She was never just looking.

She was managing. Controlling the one thing that felt controllable — information. If she knew, she couldn't be blindsided. If she was watching, nothing could sneak up on her. That was the lie she had lived inside for years.

And even now, on the other side of the marriage, she was still living in it. Still picking up the phone. Still telling herself it was practical. Still mistaking surveillance for safety.

The truth was simpler and harder to say out loud: she didn't know how to stop. She had spent years inside that marriage keeping track, paying attention, connecting dots that nobody else would connect for her. Watching had become the only way she knew how to feel safe.

And even now, with the ring off and the papers filed and Rome's consequences arriving exactly the way she always knew they would — she still didn't know how to put the phone down and trust that she didn't need to see it to survive it.

That was the part that undid her.

Not Rome. Not any of them. What undid her was realizing how much of herself she had spent. How many hours. How many nights. How many mornings she had picked up that phone before she'd even had coffee, training her nervous system to look for danger before it looked for peace.

She had done that. Nobody had made her. She had chosen vigilance over rest for so long that rest had started to feel like negligence.

She used to think love was supposed to feel like fire. Until she remembered that fire doesn't care what it destroys.

And the grief of that — the grief of what that marriage had quietly taken from her in ways she was still discovering — was different from the grief of losing Rome. Losing Rome she had already mourned. This was something else. This was mourning the version of herself who had existed before she learned to track and search and decode and prepare.

She wanted her back.

She wasn't sure yet if she was coming.

She remembered that earlier version of herself in pieces — the way she used to wake up slow, no agenda, no dread, no reaching for the phone before her eyes had even adjusted to the light. The way she could sit in a room with someone she loved and not be running a quiet background check on everything they said. The way trust had once felt like breathing — not a decision, not an act of will, just something that happened naturally because nothing had yet taught her not to.

She laughed easier. Slept harder. Gave without calculating the cost first.

She had not lost that woman all at once. Rome hadn't taken her in a single moment. She had left gradually — one night, one discovery, one filed thing at a time — until the woman who remained was sharper and more careful and better at surviving and so much lonelier than she had ever planned to be.

She is the one Celeste is choosing now, even if she's still finding her way back.

She just wanted to be loved the way she loved. That was all. That was everything.

This wasn't about Rome. It was never really about Rome. They always had him — Kelly, Erica, the others. He had been in and out of their lives long before she arrived and, it turned out, throughout the entire time she stayed. The loss of him was real, but it wasn't the deepest thing she was grieving. What she was grieving was what all of them had taken from her without ever once looking her in the face and understanding she was a full person. A woman with a life and a history and a thing she had carried quietly and trusted to the wrong man.

There are things you carry in a marriage that have no name in the ceremony. Some truths are so heavy they reshape the person who holds them. No place in the vows. Things that exist in the private space between two people — the things you only share when you have decided someone is safe enough, permanent enough, worth the weight of knowing.

She had given Rome that. Not just her love. Not just her time. Something that predated all of it — something she had carried alone for so long that sharing it with him had felt like finally being able to put something heavy down. And he had held it. And then he had treated everything else in their marriage like it was disposable. Like the weight of what she had trusted him with didn't change what he owed her or the women he entertained outside of her. Like knowing the most private thing about her and choosing her anyway didn't mean he had to keep choosing her.

That was the loss that lived underneath all the other losses. Not the betrayals. Not the women.

The carelessness.

He had been given something irreplaceable. And he had not cared what that meant.

That was what she kept returning to, in those weeks of scrolling.

Not the betrayal itself. The casualness of it. The way she had been an inconvenience in a story that had been running long before she joined it. The way the marriage had been, to most of the people in it, a temporary condition. Something to route around. Something to wait out.

She had been the only one treating it like it was permanent.

Slowly — not all at once, not with any announcement — she stopped checking.

Not because she had found peace. Not because she had decided to be the bigger person or take the high road or any of the other things people say when they want to make grace sound like a personality trait instead of something you bleed for. She stopped because she was tired. Because the scrolling had stopped giving her anything she didn't already have. Because at some point the information ceased to be information and became just pain, recycled, looking for somewhere new to land.

And because — somewhere underneath all of it, underneath the fury and the helplessness and the humiliation of having loved someone so completely while he was so casually somewhere else — she already knew everything she needed to know.

She had always known.

Knowing had been her companion for years. The thing she carried quietly while she kept choosing to stay. And now, on the other side of it, it was the only thing that still felt entirely hers.

She had been right.

About all of it.

And being right had cost her more than being wrong ever could.

Some marriages don't end in a single moment.

They end in layers — piece by piece, late night by late night, accommodation by accommodation — until one day you look up and realize the thing you were protecting disappeared a long time ago. What remains is the memory of it. And the grief that comes with finally, fully saying so.

She doesn't hate Rome.

She still thinks about him sometimes. The man he could be in the good moments. The way things felt in the beginning, when she still believed the best version of him was the truest one. That marriage lives somewhere in her memory — not as a love story, not as a failure. Just as something real. Something that shaped her. Something she survived.

Because some things you carry out of a marriage without realizing it.

And some things follow you.

The difference, she was still learning — and sooner or later, so would they.

The marriage was dead. It had died a long time ago. They killed it. But not everything died with it. These women wanted Celeste's husband so badly, never knowing the cost of becoming her was so expensive. Some debts stay silent for years. Then they come collecting. We were all *family* now, thanks to Rome spreading the wealth.

The marriage is buried. The thing it held is not.

RIP to The Millers.

*Freeing yourself was one thing, claiming ownership
of that freed self was another.*

— Toni Morrison

EPILOGUE
The Grief of Staying

Let Celeste tell you something about loving someone all the way. Not the surface kind. Not the kind you perform for other people or post about or describe in ways that make it sound manageable. She had loved the kind where you actually let go. Where you stop protecting yourself long enough to let another person in — all the way in — and you build something together that only the two of you fully understand.

That's what she thought they had.

And for a while — for a real, breathing, honest while — they did.

Before the honeymoon ended. Before the phone buzzed. Before she learned that what felt like shelter was really just the eye of the storm.

He held the parts she never showed anyone, and he didn't flinch. And she thought that meant something permanent. She thought a man who could hold your truth without dropping it was a man who would stay.

She was wrong about what holding meant. So she stayed.

She stayed when she should have looked harder. She stayed when the smoke was already curling between their words and she told herself it was just the heat of something real. She stayed because she believed in the vow. Because she had promised. Because she had stood in front of everyone they loved — twice — and said so out loud.

She filed things quietly. Explained things away. Watched him cry and let one tear be enough. Turned the car around when she should have kept driving. Carried his things back inside through the same door she had put them out of. Renewed vows with a man who was already somewhere else and told herself the words would realign something.

She confused burning with belonging.

That was her part. She owns it.

But eventually something else arrived.

Not loud. Not all at once. Just a slow accumulation of mornings where she picked up the phone before she'd had coffee, training her nervous system to look for danger before it looked for peace. A slow accumulation of nights lying in the dark beside him, knowing what she knew, choosing silence because naming it would make it real.

The anger came in waves. Some she swallowed. Some she didn't. She said things she meant. She said some things she didn't. She bit down when hands found her throat — the same hands, twice — and she told herself that grief was doing something to him he didn't know how to control. She told herself that love was supposed to feel like this. That intensity meant it was real. That holding on was the same thing as fighting for something worth keeping.

It wasn't.

Holding on was just holding on.

Then came the bargaining.

I'll stop throwing him out if he promises to honor the marriage. I'll go to counseling. I'll try again. I'll give it one more chance — one more conversation, one more trip, one more version of the words they'd already said.

She believed that if she loved him right and long enough, the man she had glimpsed in the good moments would finally become the man he was all the time.

She kept reaching for that man.

He kept not being there.

The body keeps score when the mind refuses to.

She knew that now. She knew it first from a shower floor, from a room that leaned sideways, from a diagnosis that had a clinical name for what grief and stress and a marriage that was quietly destroying her had done to her nervous system. Her therapist called it situational depression. She called it the cost of staying too long inside something that had been on fire the whole time.

She stopped being able to tell where the weight ended and she began.

Some mornings it just felt like surviving.

She decided that counted.

Rome left their marriage. She just followed.

Not because the love ran out. She wasn't sure love was ever the right word for what they had. She loved him — she knew that. But love requires two people moving toward the same thing. And Rome was always moving toward something else.

She left because she finally understood that loving someone is not the same as being safe with them. And she had spent years confusing the two, calling it devotion. Calling it commitment. Calling it what God joined together.

It wasn't devotion.

It was survival that had finally remembered its own name.

Here is what she knows now:

There is no rushing this. Grief opens on its own schedule, in its own order, and the only way out is through — slowly, without shortcuts, without forcing the timeline because she's tired of feeling it.

Her body still remembers things her mind has tried to release. She is still learning to be patient with that. It doesn't mean she hasn't healed. It means she actually loved someone. It means it was real.

He built something in her that she is still figuring out how to carry. Not damage — though there was damage. Something alongside it. A clarity. A knowledge of herself she did not have before she walked into that marriage and did not have before she walked out of it. She knows what she is made of now.

She knows what she can survive. She knows the difference between a woman who is loved and a woman who is needed, and she will never again mistake one for the other.

She wanted to be loved the way she loved.

That was all.

That was everything.

She should have walked out the door the moment she realized she wasn't. She didn't. She stayed because she loved him.

Rome never knew who he was really married to. That was his loss. And hers. She grieved him the way you grieve something that was never fully yours to begin with.

She learned — at great cost, across years, through rooms and hotel hallways and hospital beds and a front lawn scattered with her own belongings — exactly who she is. And she is worth far more than what she settled for.

She grieved what died, honored what lived, and finally chose herself.

About the Author

Sable Miles writes fiction that is emotionally raw, psychologically layered, and rooted in the kinds of truths people do not always say out loud. Her work is inspired by the emotional complexities of love, disappointment, loyalty, and the quiet ways people break and rebuild inside relationships.

With a storytelling style that is intimate, reflective, and unafraid of discomfort, she explores what happens when vows, trust, and identity begin to unravel. Her fiction speaks to readers who understand that not every ending is loud—and not every wound is visible.

The Marriage I Mourned is her exploration of grief, betrayal, and the painful clarity that comes when love and reality stop looking the same.

Sable Miles writes for readers who want stories that feel real, haunting, and emotionally unforgettable.

THE CELESTE MILLER SERIES

The Marriage I Mourned (Book One)

Karma (Book Two) — Coming Soon

Next Lifetime (Book Three) — Coming Soon

www.ingramcontent.com/pod-product-compliance
Lightning Source LLC
Chambersburg PA
CBHW032026050726
47590CB00006B/2323